"Where's your baby?"

"She's with Rae." Laurel poked a thumb over her shoulder. "I, uh, wanted to talk with you alone."

Sucking in a breath, Wes said, "Laurel, about that night—"

"Sarah-Jane is your daughter." Shoulders squared, she looked him in the eye.

As his brain struggled to comprehend what she'd said, he simply stood there for the longest time. He must not have heard her correctly. "I'm sorry. Could you please say that again?"

"No, I'm the one who should be sorry." Shaking her head, she looked suddenly frazzled. "I'm saying this all wrong." She drew in a deep breath and exhaled before tentatively meeting his gaze. "My daughter, Sarah-Jane. She's your daughter, too."

Thoughts of the frightened infant he'd tried to console yesterday sifted through his mind, stealing his breath. With all the chaos, it wasn't like he'd really gotten a good look at her. And then at the restaurant, he'd been so focused on Laurel. "Y ... ared at the woman b ... hend. "We have

It took **Mindy Obenhaus** forty years to figure out what she wanted to do when she grew up. But once God called her to write, she never looked back. She's passionate about touching readers with biblical truths in an entertaining, and sometimes adventurous, manner. Mindy lives in Texas with her husband and kids. When she's not writing, she enjoys cooking and spending time with her grandchildren. Find more at mindyobenhaus.com.

Books by Mindy Obenhaus

Love Inspired

Bliss, Texas

A Father's Promise

Rocky Mountain Heroes

Their Ranch Reunion
The Deputy's Holiday Family
Her Colorado Cowboy
Reunited in the Rockies
Her Rocky Mountain Hope

The Doctor's Family Reunion
Rescuing the Texan's Heart
A Father's Second Chance
Falling for the Hometown Hero

Visit the Author Profile page at Harlequin.com.

A Father's Promise

Mindy Obenhaus

ISBN-13: 978-1-335-48826-8

A Father's Promise

This edition published by arrangement with Harlequin Books S.A.

For questions and comments about the quality of this book, please contact us at CustomerService@Harlequin.com.

Love Inspired
22 Adelaide St. West, 40th Floor
Toronto, Ontario M5H 4E3, Canada
www.Harlequin.com

Printed in U.S.A.

Every good gift and every perfect gift is from above, and cometh down from the Father of lights, with whom is no variableness, neither shadow of turning.

—*James* 1:17

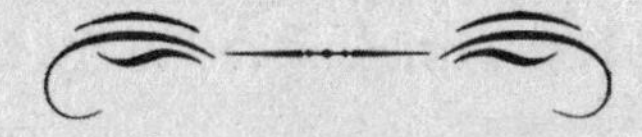

For Your glory, Lord.

Acknowledgments

To my husband, Richard. You are the greatest gift I could have been given. Thank you for loving me despite my warts, supporting my dreams and encouraging me to fly. I love you.

To Stacey Collier. Thank you for all of your input and allowing me to utilize both your career and your house for this story.

Chapter One

Laurel Donovan had no reason to be anxious. After all, she'd been contemplating this day for weeks. Yet as she maneuvered her fourteen-month-old daughter's stroller along the tree-lined streets of Bliss, Texas, Monday morning, she couldn't shake the feeling that something was about to happen. Something big and life altering.

Breathing in the crisp spring air, she cast the ridiculous notion aside and listened to Sarah-Jane's happy babble instead. Laurel had never expected to be a mother, because to do that one typically had a husband, and Laurel wasn't prone to romantic relationships. Matter of fact, they scared her. She'd had enough rejection for one lifetime.

Unfortunately, she was human. And two years ago, the only faith Laurel had was in herself. But Sarah-Jane was a perfect example of what the pastor always said about God turning even our biggest mistakes into our greatest blessings.

Being a single mother wasn't easy, though, especially when you had no family. And while Laurel's grandmama Corwin had cared for her after her mother passed away, Sarah-Jane would have no one if anything happened to Laurel. She'd become a ward of the state, and Laurel couldn't let that happen. She had to do everything in her power to make sure her daughter would be taken care of by people who loved her, whether she was with Laurel or not.

The late-April sun warmed her face as they approached Rae's Fresh Start Café in the heart of Bliss. The breakfast, brunch, lunch and specialty coffee place had become a daily staple for Laurel even before Sarah-Jane was born. No one but Rae could make decaf coffee taste as good as its caffeinated counterpart. And the amazing brew had sustained Laurel throughout her pregnancy.

Her daily visits had also provided her with three of the best friends she'd ever known. Thanks to Bliss's ad campaign to lure younger folks to the aging town, Rae, Laurel, Paisley and Christa had arrived within a year or so of each other, all looking for a new beginning. And not a one of them had ever judged Laurel for being single and pregnant. Instead, they'd embraced her, walking with her through her pregnancy and beyond. Which was why Laurel had insisted on this morning's meeting.

"G'morning, Laurel." Rusty Hoffman paused his sidewalk sweeping in front of the Bliss State Bank building. "And how is Miss Sarah-Jane doing today?" Leaning against his broom, the stocky middle-aged man with brown eyes and black hair peppered with a hint of gray smiled down at her daughter.

"Happy to be outside and on the move." Laurel pulled back the stroller's canopy to reveal a wide-eyed Sarah-Jane staring blankly at the man.

"Well, I can't say as I blame her," Rusty said. "The Lord's given us a fine morning."

"He sure has." Laurel took in the cloudless sky,

grateful that God had led her to Bliss, where bankers weren't too pretentious to sweep sidewalks and streets were built around two-hundred-year-old live oaks. Back in Dallas, they would have cut down the trees in the name of progress.

Laurel coaxed Sarah-Jane to wave goodbye before continuing across the street to the courthouse square. Brick buildings dating back to the late 1800s still lined two of the streets surrounding the square. Some had been painted in bright colors indicative of the Victorian era, while others remained in their natural state. Their charm, coupled with the ancient live oaks and magnolia trees that encircled the courthouse, were what had initially drawn Laurel to Bliss nearly two years ago.

After the death of her grandmother, a pregnant Laurel had been eager for a new beginning. Someplace she could call home. And like the town motto said, everyone needed a little Bliss in their life.

Her daughter chattered and clapped her hands as they moved off the curb to cross to the café.

"You know where we're going, don't you, baby?"

Laurel had been pondering her daughter's future almost from the moment she'd discovered she was pregnant. And after a recent bout with the flu had Laurel envisioning all sorts of horrible scenarios, she was determined to take steps to ensure her daughter would be cared for. So today was the day she was finally going to ask her friends, all of whom were single, if they would consent to raise Sarah-Jane in the event anything happened to Laurel.

Halfway across the street, the hairs on the back of her neck suddenly prickled, and a sense of dread had her feeling as though she was moving in slow motion. Then, out of the corner of her eye, she saw a red Crown Victoria rounding the corner. Another glance had her realizing it was coming straight toward her and Sarah-Jane.

She tried to run but couldn't seem to make her feet move.

"Look out!" she heard someone yell.

Fear tried to close in around her, but she couldn't allow that to happen. She had to protect Sarah-Jane.

As the car inched closer, she propelled Sarah-Jane toward the curb. The stroller had barely left her grip when the vehicle struck Laurel. She rolled onto the hood of the car, only to tumble off again when the driver slammed on the brakes a split second later.

Air whooshed out of Laurel's lungs. She lay there, momentarily dazed, the shaded asphalt cool beneath her fingers and cheek. Her breath returning, she mentally evaluated her body parts, then opened her eyes and lifted her head to see people gathering on the sidewalk.

A man with dark hair knelt beside Sarah-Jane's stroller, concern marring his handsome features as he talked to her. And he—looked familiar.

The car door creaked open then, and a woman shrieked.

"I killed her! Oh, help me, I killed her!"

Laurel knew that voice just as well as she knew the vehicle that had struck her. She rolled onto her back as the ninety-three-year-old shuffled alongside her in tennis shoes that were whiter than her hair.

"Mildred Godwin!" Laurel ground out the name.

"Ack!" The woman, who was so small she could barely see over the steering wheel, pressed a hand to her chest. "You're alive! Thank You, Lord! You're alive!"

"Mildred—" Laurel sat up, grateful the nonagenarian had a tendency to drive at a snail's pace. Though in the moment, it had seemed much faster. "—you know you're not supposed to be driving. How on earth did you get your keys? I thought your son locked them up."

"Ladies—" Drenda Kleinschmidt, owner of Bliss Antiques and Gifts and wife of Laurel's pastor, helped Laurel to her feet "—are y'all all right?" Concern filled her blue eyes as they assessed Laurel.

"I'm fine." Laurel continued to wait for Mildred to respond about the keys.

Instead, the older woman pursed her bright red lips together and looked away, suddenly sheepish.

"Mildred…?" Hands on her hips, Laurel was not about to budge until she had an answer. The woman was a hazard to the entire town.

"I—" The woman lifted one slight shoulder. "I had an extra set." She glanced at Laurel. "And my Muffy was hungry for some of that special cat food. You know, the kind they advertise being served in a crystal bowl. Muffy loves it so much, and I was all out."

"That is *no* excuse. You could have killed me *and* my daughter." The mere thought had Laurel pressing a hand to her stomach.

A siren wailed in the distance, and Mildred's hazel eyes went wide. "They're comin' for me." She latched onto Laurel's arm with a death grip. "Please, don't let them take me. I'd never survive in jail. I'm just an old woman. Please."

"Mildred, I highly doubt you're going to jail." Drenda, the epitome of a sweet spirit, wrapped an arm around the older woman and patted her frail shoulder.

Confident that Drenda could handle things from here, Laurel pried Mildred's surprisingly strong fingers from her forearm and started toward her daughter. Her steps slowed when she, again, laid eyes on the man beside the stroller.

The sun glinted off his dark hair, and when he looked up, his gaze locked with Laurel's.

Her breath caught in her throat. Why would he be in Bliss?

She absently rubbed her left temple. Maybe she'd hit her head, after all, because she was obviously seeing things.

"Laurel!" From out of nowhere, Christa and Paisley rushed toward her.

Behind them, Rae paused beside the guy at the stroller. She said something to him, then proceeded to unhook Sarah-Jane and pick her up.

"We just heard what happened." Christa's hazel eyes surveyed Laurel from head to toe. "Are you all right?"

"Yes, I just—"

Things grew quieter as the police cruiser pulled up and that obnoxious siren finally stopped.

All of this chaos was making Laurel's head swim. "I just want to see my daughter."

Paisley slid an arm around Laurel's waist. "Of course, you do, darlin'. Come on."

Christa took the lead, parting the group of onlookers who'd gathered. Unlike in Dallas, things like this didn't happen in Bliss every day, so, naturally, all of the commotion had garnered quite a crowd. By noon, the entire town would likely know what had happened, and the story would, no doubt, make the county's weekly newspaper.

"Sarah-Jane is perfectly fine." Rae bounced the child in her arms. "All the commotion had her fretting for a little bit, but that's all."

Laurel reached for her daughter and hugged her to her chest. "Thank You, God for protecting my baby." Tears spilled onto her cheeks of their own volition.

Burying her face in Sarah-Jane's neck, Laurel breathed in her sweet fragrance. Everything really was all right.

Except...

Lifting her head, she looked at Rae. "Where'd that guy go?"

"What guy?" Rae tucked a strand of brown hair that had escaped her messy-yet-oh-so-cute updo behind her ear.

"The one by Sarah-Jane's stroller. Tall, dark hair. You were talking to him."

"Oh, that was my brother Wesley." She waved a hand. "He went back to the café to keep an eye on things for me. He was actually on his way to the hardware store when he saw you push Sarah-Jane out of harm's way, and, thankfully, stop the stroller before it hit the curb. That was some quick thinking on your part, by the way."

"Wait." Laurel was growing more confused by the second. "That was your brother?"

"Wesley, yes. I told you he was coming to visit." Rae's brow puckered. "Are you sure you're okay, Laurel?"

Wesley was Wes? If that was the case, then, no, she wasn't okay. Because, unbeknownst to him, Wes was Sarah-Jane's father.

Wes Bishop needed purpose in his life, and since he'd retired from the navy two years ago, that purpose had been lacking. He wanted to help others, to serve—which was why he'd contracted with the Servant's Heart relief organization to manage their shelter construction program in Iraq. From the moment his friend and former master chief, Eddie Perkins, had presented him with the opportunity, Wes had been all in. Yet when he agreed to come to Bliss, Texas, to visit his sister, Rae, before leaving, he never imagined he'd find his past. A past void of any kind of relationship with God. Yet even though they'd known each other for only one fleeting night that never should have happened, Laurel had left an indelible impression on his heart.

He pushed through the door of his sister's café, still not quite believing what he'd just witnessed. Everything had been such a blur out on the street. The stroller, the car, the woman. Yet while he thought he recognized the voice, he hadn't been certain until Laurel's gray-green eyes collided with his. In that moment, his heart stopped as unwanted emotions washed over him. Excitement, regret… Yeah, he had enough regrets to choke a horse.

Giving himself a stern shake, he decided to keep busy by gathering up the half dozen white coffee cups that had been abandoned when the local ranchers got wind of the accident and rushed outside. According to Rae, her Fresh Start Café was their morning gathering place. Check the herd, then head to Rae's for coffee, discussions of the weather and the latest gossip.

Well, they would have had plenty to gossip about if Wes had acted on his instincts. When he realized it had, indeed, been Laurel out there, the urge to protect and comfort her had surged within him. Instead, he tamped it down and forced himself to return to the café.

Thankfully, she was all right. And her spunk was, obviously, still intact. The way she laid into that elderly driver… He couldn't help chuckling. Not that he didn't feel for the old lady, but it sounded like she had it coming.

Moving behind the antique wooden counter, a remnant of the building's former life as a saloon, he set the cups into the gray bin designated for dirty dishes, guilt tightening his gut. He should *not* have been so happy to see Laurel. Not only was he moving overseas in just a little under a month, but the woman had a baby. Something that had initially given him pause. But the little thing couldn't have been more than nine or ten months old. Not that he knew much about babies. Still, there was probably a husband in the mix. Yet that didn't stop Wes's pulse from kicking up a notch when Laurel's gaze met his. The same way it had the first time he'd met the confident—not to mention beautiful—accountant with long, honey-blond hair and eyes that sparkled when she laughed.

He grabbed a rag and returned to the now-empty table to wipe it down. He was glad Laurel had found happiness and no longer had to face the world alone. A husband, family… It fit her. And Wes respected her too much to ever reveal their secret.

Still, it might be best if he steered clear of her to prevent any awkward situations. Besides, he didn't need the onslaught of what-ifs that were bound to invade his thoughts. There were no what-ifs in his world. He'd determined a long time ago that he would never marry, never have a family… Those were things he didn't deserve. Not after what he'd done to his parents.

The café door opened, and Wes jerked his head up to see Rae and two other women bustling Laurel and her baby inside. Just what he didn't need.

"Paisley, pull out that chair for her," Rae instructed the tall redhead. "Laurel, I want you to sit down so we can make sure you truly are all right."

Still holding her child, Laurel complied. "For the thousandth time, I'm fine."

A woman with chin-length brown hair pulled out the industrial-style metal chair beside Laurel and sat down. "You say that now, but sometimes things are delayed."

"Christa is right." The other woman with long red hair and a syrupy southern drawl peered down at Laurel. "Even if there's nothing evident now, don't be surprised if you wake up sore tomorrow."

Smiling, Laurel reached for the redhead's hand. "I appreciate y'all's concern. I don't know what I'd do without you."

"All right, what can I get for everyone?" While Rae awaited orders from her three friends, Wes glanced from the exposed brick wall opposite him to the wooden stairway at the back of the space. If he were quick enough, he might be able to escape to Rae's apartment upstairs.

Just then, Rae turned his way. "Wesley, come over here. I'd like you to meet my friends."

Great.

Rag in hand, he sucked in a breath and forced his feet to move across the old wooden floor to join his sister at the front of the restaurant.

"Ladies." Nodding, he skimmed the three faces around the square table, trying not to linger on Laurel's. Still, he couldn't help noticing that she did seem a little shaken up, amplifying his concern for her well-being.

"So, Rae's little brother finally comes to Bliss." The cute no-nonsense woman with short brown hair smiled up at him. "Christa Slocum."

"Christa owns Bliss Hardware," Rae added.

"That's good to know." He rocked back on the heels of his cowboy boots. "I'm going to be helping Rae make a few changes to her apartment—painting, removing a wall—so I'll likely be paying you a visit."

"Well, I appreciate the business." Her hazel eyes drifted to Rae. "Almost as much as your sister will appreciate having that kitchen wall gone."

"That's for sure." Rae motioned toward the next woman. "This statuesque redhead is Paisley Wainwright."

More reserved than Christa, the stylishly dressed woman simply smiled. "It's nice to meet you, Wesley."

"You'll find folks lining up down here every day for some of Paisley's decadent desserts," Rae added.

Wes looked from his sister to Paisley. "Sounds like I'm in the right place, then."

"And our heroic Mama Bear—" Rae set her hands atop her friend's shoulders "—is none other than the fabulous Laurel Donovan." His doting sister reached for the baby's cheek. "Along with Sarah-Jane."

Laurel Donovan. At least he got her last name this time. Albeit her married name.

"Laurel." He nodded, not knowing what else to say. He certainly wasn't about to let on that they already knew each other.

She tilted her head, sending her long hair spilling over one shoulder as she peered up at him curiously. "It really is you." The corners of her mouth lifted ever so slightly. "For a second, I thought I'd hit my head."

"It's a wonder you didn't." A nervous smile played at his lips. "Things could have turned out a lot worse."

A baffled Rae looked from Wes to Laurel and back again. "Um, why am I getting the feeling you two already know each other?"

Laurel continued to watch him with those eyes that lived in his memory, as though studying every nuance of his face. "We met in Las Vegas a couple of years ago. We were both there for conventions."

Something Wes would never forget. Watching a frustrated Laurel plop down on the edge of that hotel pool in her all-business dress had been intriguing, to say the least.

Turning away, she continued. "I mistook him for a waiter and asked him to bring me a soda."

"Oh no." Christa put a hand to her mouth to cover a chuckle.

"In her defense," he said, "we were at the pool, and I was wearing shorts and a polo shirt. So it was an honest mistake."

"It wasn't until I attempted to pay him that I realized he was another guest." The color in her cheeks heightened, just the way it had that day by the pool.

Again, she looked up at him through those thick lashes he remembered so well. "I never dreamed that Rae's Wesley could be the Wes I'd met that day."

Hands perched on her hips, Rae continued to watch the two of them. "Yeah. Talk about a small world."

Laurel averted her attention then. "You'll have to excuse me. I think I need to go home."

"I don't like the sound of that." The redhead promptly stood to help Laurel. "Are you feeling ill? Why don't you let me drive you?"

"Just a little shaky. But a ride would be wonderful." Standing, Laurel held her daughter close and offered a weak smile. "I think I just need to rest for a little bit."

"Let me get that stroller for you." The one who owned the hardware store shot to her feet and started for the door. "Pop the hatch on your SUV, Paise." She waved toward Rae. "I'm going to head on back to the store." She continued outside, pausing to grab the stroller that now sat in front of the window and aimed it toward a silver SUV.

"Are you sure you don't want to go to the hospital and get checked out?" Rae visually scrutinized her friend.

"No, I'm okay. Just a little overwhelmed, that's all." Laurel glanced from Rae to Wes. "Thank you for coming to my daughter's aid out there."

"No problem. I'm glad I was there to help." Watching her, he wondered if she really was okay. Like her friends had said, sometimes things were delayed. She was obviously still dazed.

No wonder Rae watched her like a hawk—or an overprotective mother—until Laurel again gave Rae her full attention. "I just need to rest for a little while."

"All right, sweetie." Rae gave her a quick hug and kissed the baby's cheek. "I'll be by to check on you later."

Rae watched as the women emptied out of the shop before moving behind the counter to start a fresh pot of coffee. "I guess you and Laurel didn't stay in touch, huh?"

"Why would we?" He pushed in the vacated chairs and gave the table a quick wipe with the rag he still held. "We only met once." Not that he wouldn't have contacted her if he'd known how. Then again, with all of his regrets about that night, it was probably just as well.

"When was that again? That the two of you met."

"A couple of years ago." He started toward the counter. "Not long after I got out of the navy."

"I see." As the coffee brewed, filling the café with its enticing aroma, Rae narrowed a scrutinizing gaze on him.

"Why are you looking at me so weird?" Moving behind the counter, he handed her the rag.

One capable shoulder lifted. "No reason." She leaned her backside against the counter. "So, did anything happen after you and Laurel met, or did you just shake hands?"

He shot her a warning look. "We had dinner, all right." They were two lonely people in need of a friend. Laurel was easy to talk to. She made him smile. And stirred feelings in him that he'd never had problems ignoring before. "There's no need to worry, though. I promise not to reveal anything to her husband."

"Husband?" Rae's expression morphed into something incredulous. "Laurel isn't married."

"She's not?" Why did that bit of information spark hope inside him? "I mean, I just assumed, with the baby and all."

Rae continued to study him. "And all, huh?"

"What is up with you? Why are you giving me the third—?" Wagging a finger toward her, he dared a step closer. "Wait a minute. I don't know what kind of cockamamie ideas are rolling around that pretty head of yours, Rae, but if you're trying to play matchmaker, you can just forget it. Yes, Laurel is a sweet person. And, yes, she's attractive, but I'm not interested in a relationship with Laurel or anyone else."

Scowling, she crossed her arms over her chest. "Because you think you're not worthy of a family."

"No, because I know I'm not. Now, if you'll excuse me—" he turned and started toward the stairs "—I have a wall to destroy."

Chapter Two

Wes was in Bliss. And he was Rae's brother?

Wearing a path in the hardwood floors of her living room while Sarah-Jane played with her toys in her portable playard later that afternoon, Laurel was still trying to wrap her brain around the whole thing. All she knew was that coming face-to-face with Sarah-Jane's father was something she'd never anticipated. Not in her wildest dreams. After all, when they'd met, she was living in Dallas and he was somewhere in Florida. Yet they both ended up in the tiny town of Bliss?

Only God could orchestrate something that crazy.

But why now? Laurel had built a life for herself and her daughter, one grounded in faith. Besides, according to Rae, Wes was moving to Iraq. Not only was that another country, it was the other side of the world. How unfair would it be to tell him he had a child when he was leaving?

Shaking her head, she dropped her face in her hands. Why had she allowed that night to happen? But then, if it hadn't, she wouldn't have Sarah-Jane. And she couldn't imagine life without her.

She turned as her daughter picked up a small baby

doll and hugged it against her chest. Laurel had two regrets in her life—never having known her father, and the knowledge that Sarah-Jane would never know hers. Now Laurel suddenly had the power to change Sarah-Jane's life, to give her daughter the one thing Laurel never had. What would that look like, though? How would bringing Wes into their lives impact Sarah-Jane? She could only assume he was a Christian, given that he was working for a mission organization, but what if he wasn't?

A knock at the front door startled her. She pressed the pause button on her thoughts and crossed to the wooden door with arched glass at the top, her steps halting beside the pale blue sofa. What if it was Wes? What if he'd figured out that Sarah-Jane was his daughter? What would he say? What would he do?

Easy, it's not like you did anything wrong. You didn't deliberately keep his daughter from him.

True. Actually, there was a part of her that had always wanted to tell him. He was a nice guy. And even if he wasn't interested in being a father, he deserved the opportunity to decide that for himself.

But she hadn't been able to do that because she'd known nothing about him. Including his last name.

Another knock had her sucking in a deep breath. She took one more step and tugged open the antique door, relieved when she saw Rae on the other side.

"I came to check on you." Her curious friend held out a foam box. "And bring you some nourishment. Beef tips and noodles were today's special."

"My favorite." Smiling, Laurel swung the door wide. "You didn't have to do that."

"Yes, I did." Rae handed the food box to Laurel as she passed. "Because I need to talk to you."

Laurel's insides tightened. Rae was her best friend, and a rather perceptive one at that.

Closing the door, she went into the adjoining kitchen for a fork and napkin, while Rae scooped up Sarah-Jane.

"You should know, I grilled my brother after you left."

Laurel's steps slowed as she approached the living room. "About what?"

"Your previous meeting." Rae eased into the off-white glider near the large front window. "Look, I'm just going to cut to the chase." She settled the baby in her lap before fixing her blue eyes on Laurel. "And I'm asking this as a friend, not Wesley's sister."

Laurel nodded, her body tense as she prepared herself for— Wait, what was she preparing for? This was Rae. Her best friend. Laurel had nothing to be afraid of.

"Is my brother Sarah-Jane's father?"

Okay, so she wasn't afraid. However, she was definitely uncomfortable. Not once had she ever spoken to anyone about Sarah-Jane's father or the night she met him. All this time, she'd kept it inside. Wes was different than most guys. He hadn't gone out of his way to try to impress her or pretended to be someone he wasn't. Perhaps it was because he was a little older. Whatever it was, she'd often wished she could see him again.

But now that she had…

Nodding, she set the foam container on the small, marble-topped peninsula that separated the cooking space from the dining area. "He figured it out, didn't he?"

"Are you kidding?" Rae puffed out a laugh. "My brother assumed you were married." She smoothed a hand over Sarah-Jane's soft blond hair, lifting a shoulder. "However, after seeing him and Sarah-Jane together, and narrowing down the timeline, I had my suspicions."

Laurel released a sigh and made her way to the couch. "Her eyes definitely belong to Wes." She dropped onto the cushions, a tangled web of emotions closing in around her.

Rae turned the child to face her. "They sure do." She kissed Sarah-Jane's chubby cheek. "You sweet baby. No wonder you've always held such a special place in my heart. I truly am your aunt." The woman who had been Laurel's birthing coach and was there to see Sarah-Jane take her first breath swiped away a tear.

After a long moment, she addressed Laurel again. Yet while her gaze remained warm, it held an ache that hadn't been there before. "Are you planning to tell him?"

"Yes." Grabbing the Pray More, Worry Less pillow beside her, Laurel hugged it against her middle. "Not that it's going to be easy. I mean, 'Congratulations, you're a father' isn't something you just blurt out." Chagrin washed over her, and her insides twisted. "It wasn't like I was trying to hide it from him or anything. I mean, I had no way to get in touch with him. We didn't exchange numbers or any personal information." Just the way she'd wanted it. That was, until she was gone.

Head cocked, Rae watched her intently. "Laurel, are you afraid?"

She looked at her friend. "Not afraid—more like ashamed. That night. That wasn't like me. But my grandmother had just died, I was fed up with my boss and, I guess, I just…needed someone. Some*thing*. And I think Wes did, too."

"Yeah, you needed Jesus." Rae was nothing if not blunt, though her tone held no accusation.

"I know that now. And it was in large part because of that night that I finally found Him. As I struggled to come to terms with the reality of my pregnancy, all those things my grandmother had tried to instill in me finally sank in. For years, I kept thinking I could rely on myself. Boy, was I wrong." Restless, she tossed the pillow aside and resumed her pacing. Rubbing her suddenly chilled arms, she said, "What if Wes doesn't believe me or thinks I expect money or something? What if he doesn't want to be a part of Sarah-Jane's life?"

"I guess we'll cross that bridge when we come to it." Standing, Rae settled Sarah-Jane back among her toys. "Though, honestly, I suspect Wesley is going to have a tough time coming to terms with this new reality."

"Who wouldn't? Wes has built a life for himself. Now he's about to learn he has a child."

Rae looked uncharacteristically distressed as she approached. "Laurel, my brother believes that he doesn't deserve a family."

She halted her pacing and stared at her friend. "Why?"

"Because he blames himself for our parents' deaths."

"But that was years ago, right?"

"Between Wesley's sophomore and junior year of high school."

The ache that filled Laurel's heart was unexpected. "Oh, Rae. That is so sad."

"It really is. Because it's a lie that has dictated the rest of his life." Rae eyed the baby once more. "Maybe God can use Sarah-Jane to free him from that lie." She sniffed. "If you need me to watch her so you and Wesley can talk, just let me know."

"I will." Laurel hugged her friend, knowing she had

a monumental task before her—one that couldn't wait. She could only pray that God would give her the words Wes needed to hear.

Wes did not want to think about Laurel. Yet no matter how hard he tried, she kept invading his brain. How did she end up in Bliss? Why wasn't she married? And why had she left so suddenly yesterday? Was it because of the accident, like she said, or had his presence made her uncomfortable?

His heart twisted. While Wes would never regret meeting Laurel, he'd definitely been humbled by his actions. He'd always tried to be an honorable man. For two years he'd wished for the opportunity to apologize to Laurel. Now God had actually presented him with that chance. But when? How? At least knowing she wasn't married might make things a little easier.

"Why are you torturing yourself, Bishop?" Standing in Rae's living room, he swung his sledgehammer, knocking another two-by-four free. He'd been up before the sun, removing the Sheetrock from the wall that separated Rae's kitchen and living spaces. Something he'd intended to do yesterday, but by the time he'd moved the furniture from the living room into the spare bedroom and covered the kitchen cupboards, appliances and countertops with plastic sheeting, it had been too late to get started.

He tossed the wood aside. "You don't do relationships, remember?" Even if he did, he was moving to Iraq, so what would be the point?

As the ranchers finished their coffee downstairs at the café and headed back to their herds, Wes freed the last two-by-four and stood back to admire the new wide-open space. The living area sat at the front of the building, where a wall of windows overlooked the courthouse square and infused the space with natural light. The kitchen, however, had been closed off, leaving it dark, cramped and uninviting.

But not anymore.

"So much better." Fortunately, the exposed brick walls had remained untouched everywhere except for the bedrooms, and the original wood floor still spread throughout the entire apartment.

Now his sister had an updated space that was bright and inviting. At least, she would once he got things cleaned up and added a fresh coat of paint, anyway. After all he'd put Rae through, it was the least he could do. There weren't many young women who would put their college experience on hold to raise their sixteen-year-old brother. Yet that's exactly what Rae had done.

Regret hit him in the gut, the way it did every time he thought about Craig and Jane Bishop's untimely deaths. He was the reason they'd been on the road that night. All because he hadn't thought before he acted.

With a shake of his head, he willed the unpleasant thoughts aside, knowing he had a job to do. He'd promised Rae he'd get this done, and he would not disappoint her.

Trading his hammer for the shovel he'd tucked into the corner beside one of the windows, he started scooping up the pieces of Sheetrock that littered the tarp-covered floor as memories of Laurel again pelted his brain. At this rate, he was going to drive himself nuts. He may as well just find out where she lived and apologize already.

"Hello?" A woman's voice echoed from the back of the apartment where the stairs were located.

"In here." Turning, he saw Laurel pushing past the

plastic sheeting he'd hung over the hallway to prevent dust from leaching into the bedrooms. And his heart skidded to a stop.

While she was dressed in a simple T-shirt and jeans, her honey-blond waves swayed around her shoulders as she tiptoed through the chunks of Sheetrock that littered the kitchen floor. She sure was beautiful, but it was more than her physical appearance that made her so attractive. In their brief time together, Wes had been privileged to get a glimpse of Laurel's heart—a heart that yearned to love and be loved. So, given that she had a child, he was kind of surprised she wasn't married. Unless she was divorced, or the father was a deadbeat. Both were things that happened far too often in today's world.

"Hi." She stopped in front of him, biting her lip as though she was nervous.

He longed to say something profound, something that would put her at ease, yet all he managed was "How are you feeling?"

"I'm good." She poked at a broken piece of drywall with the toe of her short boot. "Maybe a little achy, like Paisley said." Peering up at him, she added, "But don't tell Rae I said that."

Fully aware of just how bossy his sister could be, he couldn't help smiling. "Your secret is safe with me. That is, so long as you promise to let someone know if it gets any worse."

"I promise."

He knew what he should say next. That he should apologize and let her know that, by the grace of God, he was a different man now. Yet instead of saying that, all he could muster was "Where's your baby?"

"She's with Rae." She poked a thumb over her shoulder. "I, uh, wanted to talk with you alone."

Alone? Sounded more like God was giving him a kick in the pants, urging him to say those things Wes had rehearsed in his head for the past two years each and every time Laurel crossed his mind.

Sucking in a breath, he said, "Laurel, about that night—"

"Sarah-Jane is your daughter." Shoulders squared, she looked him in the eye.

As his brain struggled to comprehend what she'd said, he simply stood there for the longest time, leaning against his shovel. He must not have heard her correctly. "I'm sorry. Could you, please, say that again?"

"No, I'm the one who should be sorry." Shaking her head, she looked suddenly frazzled. "I'm saying this all wrong." She drew in a deep breath and exhaled before tentatively meeting his gaze. "My daughter, Sarah-Jane. She's your daughter, too."

Thoughts of the frightened infant he'd tried to console yesterday sifted through his mind, stealing his breath. "But, she's so…small."

"She's fourteen months old."

That old, huh? With all the chaos, it wasn't like he'd really gotten a good look at her. And then at the restaurant, he'd been so focused on Laurel. "So you mean your—my—" He stared at the woman before him, laboring to comprehend. "We have a daughter?"

Laurel nodded. "I would have told you, but I didn't have any idea how to contact you." Her words seemed to tumble out.

Half wandering, half stumbling, he dragged the shovel behind him as he moved toward the windows and lowered himself onto the top of a five-gallon paint bucket. He had a child? How could this be? Okay, he knew how, but why? *God, You know I never wanted a family. I don't* deserve *a family.*

Laurel remained where she was, her hands clasped tightly together. "Look, I know this is a shock. And to be clear, I don't expect anything from you. I just—" one shoulder lifted ever so slightly "—thought you should know."

Half a dozen feet away, Wes just sat there, feeling as though he'd been run over by a tank. What did he do now? He didn't know the first thing about babies or being a father.

Thoughts of his own dad and the intensity with which he'd loved Wes and Rae played across his mind. Was Wes capable of that kind of love? What if he let his child down? What if he failed?

"Can I see her?" He stood, sending the shovel crashing to the floor in the process, and wondered why he'd asked that particular question. Babies had never interested him.

This is your *baby.*

Maybe so, but he wasn't sure he was worthy of her.

A slight smile touched Laurel's lips as she nodded. "She's downstairs."

He followed her out of the apartment and to the café, uncertainty knotting his entire being. Laurel had a baby. His baby. And he hadn't been there to help.

The realization made him wince. Laurel was alone. A single mom. That couldn't have been easy, and it was his fault. He'd been weak, and Laurel had been forced to live with the consequences.

The café was empty when they reached the bottom step, something he was more than a little grateful for. Rae held the child—his child, he reminded himself—

in her arms and was dancing among the tables, swaying to and fro.

She stopped when she saw them. "Aw, who's that, Sarah-Jane?"

The beautiful little girl with hair the color of honey and the same blue eyes as his smiled as her mother approached. A moment later, that smile shifted to him, flipping his insides and his entire world upside down.

Mesmerized, he continued across the wooden floor, not knowing what to do or say.

When he stopped beside the pair, Sarah-Jane reached out her hand and offered him her cookie. How could he refuse? He pretended to nibble. "Yummy, thank you."

The grinning child seemed pleased with herself. Or him. And for some reason, that mattered. Because despite having just met her, he was smitten with this pint-size charmer. Sarah-Jane was everything good in this world—innocence, pure and simple. Her only expectation was that he would accept the cookie she'd offered. In exchange, he'd offered up his heart, and she'd snatched it without question.

And in that moment, Wes knew his life had been changed forever.

Chapter Three

Laurel had told Wes that Sarah-Jane was his daughter. Now what?

She'd hung around the café for a while, allowing Wes and Sarah-Jane to interact until Sarah-Jane got fussy and the lunch crowd started to move in. Still, Laurel would never forget the look of complete awe on Wes's face when Sarah-Jane offered him her cookie. It was a moment Laurel would cherish forever.

Where did they go from here, though? And how would Wes feel further down the road when the euphoria wore off and reality set in? Sarah-Jane had been on her best, cutest behavior this morning. However, she wasn't afraid to voice her displeasure of things, either. What would Wes think when he witnessed an all-out hissy fit?

The more Laurel thought about it, the clearer it was becoming that she hadn't thought this scenario all the way through. Instead she'd been so enamored with the thought of Sarah-Jane knowing her father, not to mention overwhelmed by yesterday's hullabaloo, that she'd simply acted.

Because you thought you were doing what was best for your daughter.

"Mah!" Sarah-Jane hollered from her playard in the living room.

Laurel looked up from the potatoes she was peeling for dinner and peered over the kitchen counter to see her daughter holding on to the side of the hexagon-shaped enclosure with one hand and a set of toy keys in the other. "What is it, baby?" At fourteen months, Sarah-Jane had mastered pulling up, but she had yet to show any real interest in walking.

Her daughter jabbered, a smile teasing at her slobber-covered lips as she watched Laurel.

"Let me get these potatoes on to boil and I'll come play with you, okay?"

The meat loaf Drenda had dropped off earlier was already in the oven, and it smelled divine. However, the green beans and corn she'd brought to accompany it weren't quite enough to properly round out this meal. With the stress of these last two days, Laurel needed some serious comfort food. And potatoes always topped that list. Mashed, with lots of butter and a little bit of cream cheese, just the way Grandmama used to make them. Besides, they were Sarah-Jane's favorite, too.

Her daughter chattered some more before plopping down on her bottom and moving on to the next toy.

Laurel felt beyond blessed to have so many people thinking of her. Last night's dinner had been courtesy of one of the ladies at church, and another friend had dropped by with a big ol' chocolate sheet cake. Laurel was almost ashamed to admit that she'd polished off nearly a third of it already. Perhaps she should consider putting the rest of it in the freezer. Less tempting that way.

She swapped her peeler for a knife and cut the russets into chunks, her thoughts drifting back to Wes. She'd done the right thing in telling him about Sarah-Jane. Unfortunately, the move had left her with a lot of uncertainty, too. Something she hadn't anticipated.

Suddenly there were so many things to consider. Things that had never crossed her mind before. Until yesterday, she'd never expected to see Wes again. Throw in the fact that he would be leaving soon to go to Iraq, and she wasn't quite sure how to approach this whole situation.

She tossed the potatoes into a pot and set it under the faucet to fill. Did Wes even want a role in his daughter's life? And how would Laurel handle that? After all, until now, it had only been her and Sarah-Jane. Yes, she wanted Sarah-Jane to know her father, but that would also mean entrusting her daughter to someone who was, for all practical purposes, a stranger. It wasn't just about him getting to know Sarah-Jane. He and Laurel had to get to know one another, too. They'd need to discuss expectations and boundaries.

There you go assuming again.

She huffed out a frustrated breath, set the pot atop the stove and turned the burner on high. The only way she'd know for sure about Wes's intentions was to ask him. And that might be even more difficult than telling him he had a daughter, because she'd probably come off sounding like a dictator.

The jingle of her phone had her glancing toward the counter, where Irma's name appeared on the screen. Despite the fact that Irma was old enough to be Laurel's grandmother, the two had forged a friendship. Probably because Irma reminded Laurel of her grandmother.

"Hi, Irma."

"Hello, Laurel. How are you feeling this afternoon?" Irma had called early this morning to check on her, too. Laurel had been tied up in knots about telling Wes and definitely hadn't been herself, which was probably why Irma called again.

"About five pounds heavier, thanks to that cake of yours. What were you thinking, bringing me the entire pan?"

Irma chuckled. "Baking for others brings me joy." As with many of the women in the church, cooking was Irma's love language.

"I know, but it's just me and Sarah-Jane. And I'm trying to be a responsible parent and teach my daughter good eating habits."

"What about your eating habits?"

Laurel frowned. "Completely uncontrolled when it comes to your chocolate sheet cake. I don't know what your secret is, Irma, but it's no wonder everyone clamors for it at church potlucks."

"Well, I'm pleased to hear you're doing better. You gave us all quite a scare."

"Don't blame me. It was Mildred Godwin—"

A knock sounded at the door.

"Irma, I'll have to call you back. Someone's here."

Ending the call, she quickly added a lid to the pot before padding to the door in her bare feet. "Who do you suppose it is, baby?" Perhaps someone was bringing more food.

Sarah-Jane abandoned the shape sorter she was playing with and pulled herself up again, seemingly as curious as Laurel.

When Laurel opened the door, she didn't have to pretend her surprise at seeing Wes on her front porch. And, man, did he look good. The torn, dust-covered jeans and paint-spattered T-shirt he'd had on earlier had been replaced with a pair of stone-colored trousers and a nicely fitted dark gray polo.

"Wes." Laurel clung to the doorknob as though it was a lifeline. If nothing else, at least it would prevent her from falling when her knees decided to buckle.

"May I come in?"

"Yes, of course." Closing the door behind him, she did her best to calm her suddenly flailing nerves. *Stop acting like a teenager.*

With blue eyes so much like his daughter's, he took in the living room of her little bungalow. "Nice place you've got here."

"Thank you." She instinctively scanned the room, grateful it wasn't too much of a mess. "It's a work in progress." With Drenda's help, she was slowly but surely getting things to look the way she wanted.

Still standing behind the couch, Laurel could tell the instant Wes's gaze landed on Sarah-Jane. The sudden smile that spread across his face warmed her heart.

"Is she walking?"

She watched her daughter. "No, not yet. But we're getting close."

Shifting from one foot to the next, Wes ran a hand through his damp dark hair as he faced Laurel. "Look, I have a ton of things I want to say to you, but I guess the biggest thing is, I'm sorry. I allowed one of the best nights of my life to be tarnished with regret because of my actions." His focus again drifted to Sarah-Jane. "And altered your life forever."

Laurel blinked, feeling rather dumbfounded. Yet while there was a lot to unpack in Wes's statement, there was only one thing he needed to know. "My life wasn't just altered, Wes, it was transformed. Learning

I was pregnant brought me to my knees, and that was precisely where God needed me to be."

One corner of his mouth lifted as he regarded her. "Interesting. Because God used that night to set me on a different path, too. A path that led me not only to Him, but back to you." He cast a glance toward his daughter. "And Sarah-Jane." Drawing in a deep breath, he again met Laurel's gaze. "There's just one problem."

She studied his face. The square jawline, the barely there stubble that darkened his chin. "What's that?"

"I can't be Sarah-Jane's father."

The words had Laurel recoiling as indignation sparked to life, simmering in her gut. And here she'd thought he was different. That he might actually care that he had a daughter. But he was no different than Jimmy Donovan, the man who had turned his back on Laurel when she was just a baby.

Crossing her arms over her chest, she felt her nostrils flare. "Can't or won't?" In that instant, the reality of his words smacked her upside the head. Was he insinuating someone else had fathered her daughter?

That simmer turned into a full, rolling boil. "Wait a minute, are you calling me a liar?"

Wes had stood face-to-face with the enemy on the streets of Iraq and numerous other places around the globe, yet even then he hadn't been shaking in his boots the way he was right now.

Frustration coursed through every fiber of his being as he searched for a way to redeem himself. He had never been good at expressing his feelings. And his propensity for making a mess of things was on full display.

Laurel continued to glare at him, and he couldn't say

he blamed her. The way his words had come out would have offended anyone.

"Not that it really matters." Her chin jutted out defiantly. "Sarah-Jane and I have done just fine without you."

He was certain the comment was intended to hurt him, and she had definitely succeeded.

Lowering his head, he desperately tried to gather his thoughts and prayed he would verbalize them correctly. "Laurel, I—"

"Why don't you just leave?" She brushed past him and he could almost feel the steam radiating from her as she yanked the door open again. "I can't believe you would come into *my* house and insult me in front of *my* daughter." When she looked up at him, he saw fire flaring in her gray-green eyes. "And to think, all this time I thought you were an honorable man."

Wes scrubbed a hand over his face. He was going about this all wrong. "Laurel, please." Standing in front of the open door, he stared down at her, imploring her to listen to what he was really trying to convey. "I was not trying to insult you. The only thing I'm guilty of is shoving my big, fat foot in my mouth."

"Congratulations, it seems to fit quite well." With one hand still on the door, she sneered.

He sucked in a breath. *Lord, help me out here. Please?* "Look, communication is not my forte, all right. What I was trying to tell you is that I don't know *how* to be a father." His heart thundered against his ribs until Laurel's stance became slightly less rigid. "I never imagined I would ever have a child of my own. I don't know how to care for a baby, or even how to change a diaper. I'm clueless, Laurel."

"Well, welcome to the club." She eased the door

closed, and he breathed a sigh of relief. "You know, Sarah-Jane didn't come with an owner's manual telling me what I was supposed to do. Before she was born, I'd never been around babies, either. See that bookcase over there?" She pointed to the wall at the far end of the living room and the shelves flanking the empty fireplace. "It's full of nothing but baby books, so feel free to borrow—"

A loud hissing sound echoed from the other room, and a look of panic flitted across Laurel's face.

"Oh no!" She rushed into the adjacent kitchen.

The urgency in her voice had him following her into the small, partially open space with white cabinets and marble countertops.

Pausing near the short peninsula that separated the cooking area from the dining, he traced the sound to a pot that was boiling over on the stove. Yet, for some reason, Laurel just stood there watching it, as though she wasn't quite sure what to do.

Moving past her, he turned off the electric burner, then grabbed a towel from the counter and transferred the pot to another burner as Sarah-Jane whimpered from the living room. Poor kid. Between this chaos and their elevated voices, they'd probably scared her.

"You get Sarah-Jane," he said, "and I'll take care of this."

While Laurel stepped away to see about their daughter, Wes grabbed a dishcloth from the stainless steel sink and started wiping up the starchy water that now covered a good portion of the stovetop.

"You don't have to do that."

He turned to find Laurel standing behind him, holding Sarah-Jane. And all eyes seemed to be on him. "It's only fair since I was the one who distracted you."

Her expression was much softer now. "You know, being a parent isn't so different than what you're doing right now."

He rinsed the cloth under the faucet. "What do you mean?" Turning off the water, he resumed his wiping.

"You saw a problem, and you addressed it."

Though he tried to follow her train of thought, he was still lost. "What does that have to do with parenting?"

"Well, when a diaper is dirty or wet, you change it. And trust me, there is a slight trick to that, but it's not rocket science."

Setting the rag beside the sink, he leaned against the countertop, unable to stop the soft chuckle that escaped his lips.

"When Sarah-Jane is hungry, I feed her. When she's thirsty, I give her a drink."

Sarah-Jane turned from watching him then and looked at her mother, all the while rubbing one hand in a rough circular motion over her chest.

"What is she doing?" Wes had never seen that before.

"She must have heard me say *drink*." Laurel gave the child her full attention. "Do you want a drink?"

There went the rubbing again.

"This—" looking at Wes, Laurel mimicked Sarah-Jane's motion "—is sign language for *please*. She's telling me she wants a drink."

"No kidding." He'd never heard of an infant using sign language. "How did you figure that out?"

"I taught her."

She moved Sarah-Jane onto the opposite hip. "This means *more*." She tapped the tips of her fingers on both hands together. "And this means *all finished*." She awkwardly waved her hands in the air.

Sarah-Jane must have been amused by her mother's actions, because she giggled and bounced.

"All right, baby. I will get you your drink." Laurel slid Sarah-Jane into her high chair beside the table before retrieving a lidded cup from beside the sink. "Of course, there are a few other things that are imperative to parenting." She moved to the refrigerator and filled the cup from the dispenser while Wes's entire body tensed.

He just knew these were going to be the things he'd never be able to live up to. "And they are…?"

"Well, trusting God to get you through it all is number one." She twisted the cup's lid on. "Because there will be days when nothing goes right."

Rubbing the back of his neck, he said, "Hmm, I can't relate to that at all."

She laughed then, the sound putting him at ease. "And then there's love." She continued toward the table and handed the cup to Sarah-Jane. "Kids need to know that they're loved unconditionally. That no matter what they do, there's someone who still cares and they can count on to be there for them."

"Like your grandmother was for you."

Turning, Laurel looked up at him, blinking. "I can't believe you remembered that."

"There's not much you said that night that I don't remember." Probably because he'd replayed it over and over in his mind for the past two years.

A smile tilted the corners of her pretty lips. "You were a good listener, and that was what I needed."

"I guess I was blessed to be in the right place at the right time."

She nodded. "Now here we are again."

"With a daughter, no less." He winked at the precious child they'd unwittingly created. "So, where do we go from here?"

"I've been wondering the same thing." She leaned against the French door that led outside. "I suppose we could discuss our predicament over supper. That is, if you'd care to join us?" Laurel glanced toward the stove. "Assuming it's still edible."

His gaze drifted to the beautiful child he'd never known existed. "I think I'd like that very much."

Chapter Four

Laurel woke up Wednesday morning feeling a sense of relief. Wes hadn't rejected her daughter. However, his text message at eight thirty this morning, asking her to meet him at the café, had her wondering if he'd changed his mind. His message had been short and to the point. Not nearly as friendly and forthcoming as the man who'd had dinner with them last night.

While they enjoyed Drenda's meal, Wes had asked question after question about Laurel's pregnancy, Sarah-Jane's birth and her first year, as though wanting to know everything he'd missed. He'd even broached the topic of child support, saying he wanted to care for his daughter in every way, including financially. Later, he and Sarah-Jane had played while Laurel cleaned up the kitchen. All in all, it had been an unexpected yet pleasant evening. For all practical purposes, Wes was the same friendly, easygoing guy she'd met two years ago.

But his text was different. Strictly business. So, as she parked Sarah-Jane's stroller outside Rae's place, anxiety pulsed through Laurel's veins. If Wes turned his back on her daughter, she would…

A sigh escaped. She would go on just the way she

had before he came to Bliss. Except she'd be carrying the ache of her daughter's rejection right along with her own.

The morning air was already warm as she lifted Sarah-Jane out of the stroller. They continued inside, where the enticing aroma of coffee beckoned Laurel toward the counter.

"Good morning." Rae smiled as they approached. "And how is the most adorable little girl ever doing this morning?" She leaned across the counter to give Sarah-Jane a kiss.

The child grinned and reached for Rae, who readily obliged.

"Happy to see you, apparently." Laurel glanced around the restaurant, noting four ranchers still nursing their morning ritual and a couple of other folks enjoying a late breakfast, but no Wes.

"He's upstairs." Rae's perceptiveness really bugged Laurel sometimes. It was almost impossible to get anything past her. "Told me to let you know he'd be down in a minute."

"Good." Laurel faced her friend. "Just enough time for you to whip up my usual."

"You got it." She passed Sarah-Jane back to Laurel. "Better check out Paisley's pastry offerings before they're all gone."

"Ah..." As Rae set to work on Laurel's Americano, Laurel shifted her attention to the chalkboard that hung on the exposed brick wall behind the counter, ignoring the fact that she had almost half of a chocolate sheet cake at home. "Strawberry cupcakes, oatmeal-cranberry cookies and her Blissfully chocolate brownies." All grab-and-go treats. Just the way folks liked it. They could stop in, pick up some goodies and be on their way.

"Laurel, I'm glad you're here."

She turned as Wes approached, wearing a gray Navy Seabees T-shirt and faded jeans, her desire for sweets waning. The pucker in his brow and the laptop in his hands said this meeting was, indeed, strictly business—at least until his gaze shifted to Sarah-Jane and a smile blossomed.

"May I?" He set his computer on a nearby table and held out his hands as though he wanted to hold her daughter.

"Uh, yeah. Sure." She didn't have to coax Sarah-Jane, who readily leaned into her father's waiting arms, a sight Laurel found as endearing as she did troubling. "What did you want to talk about?"

Her phone rang before Wes had a chance to respond. She tugged it from the back pocket of her jeans and looked at the screen. Irma. She must be calling to check on Laurel again. Yet as she started to tuck the phone away, something urged her to answer.

"Excuse me," she said before swiping her finger across the screen and placing the phone to her ear. "Irma, can I call—"

"Help me, Laurel! My house is caving in!" Laurel's worries about Wes faded into oblivion as her heart skidded to a stop. Irma wasn't one to make mountains out of molehills.

"What do you mean?"

"I was in the kitchen washing up my breakfast dishes when I heard this horrible crash. The upstairs bathroom is in my family room."

Concern coursed through Laurel. "Irma, are you all right?"

"I'm not hurt, but I have no idea what to do." Irma's normally calm voice trembled. "There's water everywhere, and it just keeps coming. I'm outside on the porch, and I don't know what to do. I need help, Laurel."

"Don't worry, Irma." Her gaze drifted to Wes. "I'll be right there."

Ending the call, she relayed the information to Rae and Wes.

"That's a pretty old house." Rae handed Laurel her drink before glancing toward her brother. "There's no telling what could have happened."

"How does a house just cave in?" Laurel inadvertently deferred to Wes, knowing he was in the construction business.

"I won't know until I see it. But I suggest we get over there now." Moving around the counter, he passed Sarah-Jane into his sister's waiting arms.

Uncertainty had Laurel lifting a brow. "We?"

"Yes. I want to make sure things are structurally sound before you step inside that house."

The impact of his words wound around her heart. It was as though he cared about her.

"Come on." He started toward the door while Laurel simply watched him.

At least, until Rae motioned for her to follow. "I'll keep Sarah-Jane, you just go."

"We'll take my truck." Wes pointed toward the charcoal-gray pickup as she raced outside under the midmorning sun.

"Considering I walked, that seems like the best option." She hopped into the passenger seat as he climbed behind the wheel.

Starting the engine, he glanced her way. "Not to mention that I have tools. And with water spewing, it's likely I'll need them."

"Good point."

After checking to make sure things were clear behind him, he backed into the street. "Which way am I going?"

"Make a right at the corner." She watched him across the cab. The determined set of his jaw. Wes was one of those guys who approached things sensibly, without getting wound up. Unflappable, as her grandmother used to say. But Laurel had certainly thrown him for a loop when she told him about Sarah-Jane. And, as far as she was concerned, the jury was still out on the outcome of that situation. "Take another right up here."

It wasn't that she didn't want to trust Wes, she just wasn't sure she could. Just like she couldn't trust her mother whenever she promised that things would be different. Aside from Rae, Christa and Paisley, Grandmama was the only person who'd ever earned Laurel's trust. She had been the one constant in Laurel's life. When Brenda and Jimmy Donovan turned their backs on Laurel, Grandmama was always there with a warm embrace and fresh-baked cookies.

Two minutes later, Wes eased the truck to a stop in front of the pale yellow Victorian with white trim where Irma paced the graceful front porch, wringing her hands.

Wes let go a low whistle. "That's a lot of house for one person."

Laurel reached for the truck's door handle. "Maybe, but it's been in her family for over a hundred years." She slid onto the curb, tossing the door shut behind her before rushing up the walk to her friend.

The eighty-year-old, who had more spunk than most people half her age, met Laurel at the top step, her brown eyes brimming with unshed tears. "My beautiful house is ruined, Laurel."

Unable to stop herself, Laurel wrapped her arms around the petite, silver-haired woman. "I'm so sorry." She held her for a moment before releasing her. "I brought a friend with me, Irma." Motioning Wes closer, she continued. "This is Rae's brother, Wes. He knows all about construction, so he's going to take a look at things."

Irma lifted her wire-framed glasses to wipe her eyes. "Oh, thank you."

"Laurel says there's a water leak."

Depositing the tissue into the pocket of her baggy pants, Irma said, "More like Old Faithful. Go see for yourself." She poked an arthritic thumb toward the door. "The whole house is liable to float away."

Wes nodded. "I'm on it."

"Irma, you wait out here," said Laurel. "I'm going to go with him."

"All right, but you be careful. I wouldn't want to be responsible for leaving that sweet little girl of yours without a mama."

Laurel's heart cinched as she inched toward the screen door. Could it really be that bad?

Wes waited at the entrance. "I told you I wanted to check things out first."

"And I said I'm going with you." Fists firmly planted on her hips, she dared him to argue.

After a long moment, he creaked open the screen door and moved into the dimly lit entry hall.

"The family room is straight ahead." Following close behind, she pointed beyond the staircase that hugged the wall to their right.

"I can hear the water."

"Me, too." Glancing to her left, she found the parlor

and all of its vintage furnishings untouched. "That's probably not good, though, is it?"

"No, it's not." He stopped halfway down the hall, aiming a flashlight she didn't even know he had at the longleaf pine floors. "And it's already made it this far."

Looking down, she noted the water spreading in every direction. Her anxiety heightened as Wes picked up his pace and continued into the family room.

As her eyes adjusted, a sick feeling seized Laurel's stomach. "Oh no." She turned this way and that, trying to take it all in. "This is horrible." Bits of plaster and shards of wood floated over the floor, and a commode lay shattered in front of the antique bookcase that lined one wall. Not far from the toilet, a claw-foot tub lay on its side in front of the window. Meanwhile, water poured from the second floor like a faucet.

Wes aimed his light overhead, moving it right and left. "Pipes are broken. I gotta get this water turned off." Doing an about-face, he urged Laurel back toward the front door and onto the porch. "Irma, where's your water cutoff?" He was already down the steps.

"Somewhere between the sidewalk and street." She pointed toward the narrow section of grass. "It's bad, isn't it?" Laurel could feel Irma watching her as Wes retrieved something from his truck.

"It certainly is a mess." She turned her attention to the older woman. "One that seems insurmountable at the moment, but, I promise, we'll get it figured out."

Irma shook her head, her expression pinched. "I guess this is what insurance is for."

Laurel couldn't stop the laugh that puffed out. "Yes, this is definitely what insurance is for." Slipping an arm around the woman's shoulders, she pondered all that would need to be done. Starting with a call to Irma's insurance agent and a water-removal company. She was also going to need a place to stay until the repairs were complete. No telling how long that would to take, so Laurel should probably contact the church, too.

A breeze swept over her bare arms as she gave her friend a squeeze. "Don't you worry, Irma. I'm going to see to it everything is taken care of." If only she could say that about her situation with Wes. She still had no clue why he'd asked to meet with her this morning. And, at the moment, it didn't look like she was going to find out anytime soon.

Between Laurel's accident and the debacle at Irma's, Wes was starting to see that his vision of Bliss being a quiet little town was sorely misguided. Then again, if his time in the military had taught him anything, it was that there were struggles everywhere.

After turning off the water, he'd gone back inside Irma's supersize Victorian home to try and get a better handle on not only the cause of the collapse, but the extent of the damage. Unfortunately, the water only added insult to injury. Water had a way of reaching in, around and under everything in its wake. And the longer it remained, the more damage it would do. He suspected that at least half of the books on the shelves, many of which looked as though they could be antiques, were already damaged.

Now, while Laurel remained outside with Irma, making phone calls, Wes stood atop an old wooden ladder he'd found in Irma's garage, staring into the gaping hole in the ceiling with the aid of his flashlight and trying to figure out what had happened. Houses didn't simply collapse. There had to be a cause.

He studied the joists, in particular. While most appeared perfectly normal, other areas looked as though they'd suffered extensive water damage, making him wonder if there could have been a leak somewhere. Given the condition of the wood, it must have gone on for a long period of time. It was likely a slow leak no one had ever noticed because the wood soaked it up.

As he continued his examination, he noted the mud-like coating following the grain of the wood. A sure sign of termites. He swept the area with his flashlight. Between the water leak and the termites, the integrity of the wood must have deteriorated significantly. And when you've got something as heavy as a cast-iron tub and a toilet full of water, well, it's only a matter of time.

The good news, if one wanted to call it that, was that repairs shouldn't take more than a few weeks. No matter what, though, the first thing they had to do was get all of this water out of here so things could start drying out.

"Wes?" Laurel's voice echoed down the entry hall.

He stepped off the ladder into a puddle and met her as she entered the room with Irma and two men. "Right here."

"Oh, good." Motioning to the first man, she said, "This is Dwight Chastain, Irma's insurance agent."

Wes couldn't hide his surprise. "You got here quick."

The burly fellow with light brown hair and a goatee chuckled. "My office is only a couple of blocks away. And when there's water involved, we certainly don't want to waste any time."

"That's for sure." Wes eyed the other man clad in jeans, a chambray work shirt and a dirty ball cap.

"Mason Krebbs." Younger and leaner than the first guy, Mason held out his hand and Wes took hold. "I'm a local contractor."

"Mason was at the office when Laurel called," said

Dwight. "Thought it might be a good idea to bring him along. You know, get a contractor's perspective."

"Actually, Wes is a construction manager," Laurel was quick to point out, obviously unimpressed by Mason's credentials. Slipping her hands into the pockets of her skinny jeans, she added, "He's also Rae's brother, and he's been on top of things since we got here."

While Laurel remained beside a distressed Irma, the two men moved deeper into the room, scanning floor to ceiling.

"Were you able to find anything?" Dwight craned his neck, eyeing the six-foot chasm overhead.

"Yes, sir. There are definite signs of both water and termite damage."

Mason climbed the ladder to do his own investigation. "While I'm not necessarily one to disagree, Wes, termites and water damage don't usually result in something this drastic. I mean, wouldn't ol' Irma have noticed some weak areas in the bathroom floor or seen water spots on the ceiling?"

"I don't recall any water spots," said Irma. "And I'm in here all the time. I don't usually go upstairs, though. Only if I'm going to have company, and then it's only long enough to change out the sheets and the towels."

"From the looks of things, this has been going on for a prolonged period of time," added Wes. "We're talking years."

"Yeah, I can definitely see termite trails," Mason conceded. "They sure made a mess of this old wood." Stepping down, he addressed the agent. "The remaining wood will need to be treated for termites before new joists are added. Then the whole bathroom will likely need to be redone, the ceiling down here replaced and whatever damage was done by all this water fixed." He motioned toward the floor. "May need some new Sheetrock, carpet… And if we don't get this wood dried out right away—"

"Hello?" A woman's voice filtered down the hall.

"That's Christa." Laurel hurried to the doorway and waved her friend in.

Sporting jeans and a bright blue Bliss Hardware T-shirt, Christa stepped into the room. "Whoa. What a mess." She hugged Irma. "I'm so glad you weren't hurt." Releasing the older woman, she took in the other faces. "Wes." She nodded. "Dwight. Mason." Her attention returned to Laurel. "I've got a shop vac in the truck, along with three air movers. And there are at least three other people who will also be dropping off shop vacs. The faster you can get things dried out—"

"Her insurance will pay to bring in a water-removal company from the city."

Christa looked at Dwight very matter-of-factly. "That's fine and dandy, but they're not here now. And by the time they are, we could have most of this water squared away. The longer it sits, the more damage it's going to do."

Wes found himself slightly amused by the exchange. "Like you said, Dwight, when there's water involved, we don't want to waste any time. However, we will need a dumpster of some sort, because once you've gathered whatever information you need—taken pictures and such—we'll start emptying all of the impacted rooms, and we're going to need someplace to put this debris."

"That's right. And my guys and I could probably get started on the reconstruction in a week or so." Mason appeared to study the situation. "Shouldn't take us more than six weeks to get 'er done."

"Six weeks?" Wes, Laurel, Christa and Irma said collectively.

Wes knew it wouldn't take anywhere near that long. Especially with a crew. Sounded like Mason was just trying to pad his wallet by stretching things out.

"Where on earth will I stay?" Irma's bottom lip trembled.

Wes hated that this guy was trying to take advantage of her. He wasn't even sympathetic.

"We could try for five," Mason countered. "It's hard to tell until you get going on things, though." He smiled as if everything was just peachy. "I'll drop off an estimate later."

The man had barely even assessed things.

"Right now, though, I need to run. Can't keep the little woman waiting."

No, but he sure didn't have any problem making Irma wait.

Mason touched the brim of his ball cap before strutting back down the hallway. "Howdy, Ms. Parsons."

"Mason, you'd better not be here to take advantage of my friend."

Laurel and Wes exchanged a look as a white-haired woman eased into the room with a large multicolored purse dangling from one elbow.

She tsked several times as she took in the room. "This is quite a mess."

"It's more than a mess, Joyce," said Irma. "It's horrible. They're telling me I can't stay here."

"Well, of course you can't. Anyone can see that. So you may as well pack your bags."

"I don't know where I'd go." Irma continued to wring her hands.

"I have three empty bedrooms. You just take your pick."

"Oh, that is so sweet of you, Joyce."

"No, it's just one problem solved. Now—" the woman waved an arm "—what are you going to do about the rest of this?" Her gaze landed on Wes then, and narrowed. "Who are you?"

He cleared his throat. This woman was more intimidating than most of his superiors in the navy. "Wes Bishop, ma'am."

She moved closer, not the least bit intimidated by the standing water. "You're not from around here, are you?"

"No, ma'am. Rae Girard is my sister. I'm here to visit her."

"How come the two of you have different last names?"

"Rae was married. Her ex-husband was a Girard."

She peered up at him through her bifocals. "I like Rae. And I like that you say *ma'am*. You have manners."

He found himself standing at attention. "Twenty years in the military will do that."

"What branch?"

"Navy."

"My husband served in the navy." Taking a step back, she continued to size him up. "I'm Joyce Parsons." She smiled then. "You know I'm messing with you, right?"

"Yes, ma'am." Okay, he may have fibbed a little on that one.

"Good." She looked at the others now. "So, what's the plan, Dwight?"

The man appeared more than a little nervous. "We're going to get Irma fixed up just as quick as we can."

"And how quick is quick?" Hands clasped, Joyce waited.

"Mason said six weeks."

"Mason doesn't know his head from a hole in the ground," she said. "He's an opportunist."

Wes was liking Joyce more all the time. And he was certain that Mason's bid would be ridiculously high. Yet while Wes was more than capable of handling the job himself, he was only in Bliss for three weeks. He might be able to do it, providing any subs he'd need—termite people, a plumber and flooring people—were available. Worst-case scenario, he could do the flooring himself, but a licensed plumber was a must. As was the termite treatment. And if any of these wood floors had to be refinished, that would take time Wes didn't have.

He looked at Irma again, his heart going out to the poor woman. *Lord, what should I do? I'd hate to let her down.*

What if he wasn't able to finish the job before it was time to leave? Then again, if the downstairs was complete, Irma could still move back in. And if he had folks lined up to handle those final details of plumbing and flooring, perhaps Laurel could oversee them.

He caught Laurel's eye. "Could I see you outside for a minute?"

She nodded, then looked at the others. "Excuse us, please."

They moved down the hall, through the screen door, across the porch and onto the lawn before he said anything.

"I want to help Irma." He shoved a hand through his hair, eyeing the sprawling tree branches overhead. "I'm just not sure I can."

"Wes, you don't have six weeks."

"No, but I have almost three. And the job shouldn't take any more than that." He looked her in the eye. "It just depends on how long it takes us to get things out of here and dry before the work can begin."

"I've already contacted the church. The pastor is out of town, but Roxanne, the church secretary, is lining up volunteers to help us move stuff right now. I told her I would oversee things."

Wes couldn't help frowning. "Why would you do that? What about Sarah-Jane?"

"Because Irma is my friend, and her kids all live out of state. Besides—" she lifted a shoulder "—she reminds me of my grandmother."

Given that Laurel had thought the world of her grandmother, that statement explained a lot.

"As far as Sarah-Jane, I'll figure it out. Rae's keeping her for the rest of today, though."

He stared at the determined woman whose long hair was now pulled back into a ponytail. "You're familiar with the area. Could you help me find a plumber and termite people?"

"Sure. Brandt Hefley goes to my church. He's a plumber. And he has a big heart. I have no doubt he'd be more than happy to help Irma."

"Good."

She watched him. "So, are you going to extend the offer?"

He couldn't help grinning. "Well, as my old buddy Eddie would say, some things are worth fighting for." He nodded toward the house. "I can't let that Mason fellow take advantage of her."

"Who's Eddie?"

"He was my boss in the navy, then I went to work for him again after I retired. He's the reason I was in Vegas. But he also got me back into the church and become my spiritual mentor. He's the one who recruited me for Servant's Heart."

"Sounds like a very special friend."

"I'm blessed to know him."

Laurel's expression softened, a smile teasing at her pretty lips. "Shall we go see what Irma thinks then?"

He motioned toward the house. "Lead the way."

Chapter Five

Laurel had never ached so much in her entire life. Here she'd thought lugging a fourteen-month-old around was keeping her fit. She was obviously delusional, because removing everything from the impacted areas at Irma's had taken its toll. The debris, furniture, books… It had taken a group effort to move that old cast-iron tub out to the front porch.

God had provided them with lots of help, though. No fewer than ten people had chipped in throughout the day, helping them empty the affected rooms and move as much as they could into the parlor and dining room. Since water had leached into Irma's bedroom, soaking the carpet, it had been lifted and the pad cut away. Wes had removed all of the baseboards so no water would be trapped. Then, with the aid of shop vacs, they'd managed to rid the place of any standing water. By the time the water-removal crew Dwight had insisted they call in arrived from the city, all they had to do was add a few more air movers to the mix to speed up the drying process.

The only break they'd taken was when a group of women from the church brought them all King Ranch casserole and peach cobbler for dinner. Considering Wes and Laurel had skipped lunch, that meal was a welcome treat.

Now, as Laurel sat in the cab of Wes's pickup with a country music station playing low on the radio, she was almost too numb to think. All she wanted was to get home, hug her baby girl and crawl into bed. Then she recalled how her day had started—with Wes asking her to come to the café to discuss something. She still didn't know what that something was. And while she was appreciative for all Wes had done today—his take-charge attitude and offering to do the repairs to Irma's house—Laurel's heart was weighted down by that one unknown. Because it could determine the course of her daughter's future.

The sun was low on the western horizon, shading the tree-lined streets of Bliss as they made their way back to Laurel's where Rae waited with Sarah-Jane. Looking at Wes, Laurel couldn't help noticing that he didn't appear anywhere near as exhausted as she felt. Then again, he was probably used to this sort of stuff. Honestly, she was glad he'd been with her today. She might know how to organize a work crew, but she knew nothing about building.

Knowing they were only minutes away from her house, she mustered her courage. "What was it you wanted to talk to me about this morning?"

He shook his head and gave a slight smile. "So much has happened since then, I'd almost forgotten."

Great. While she couldn't say she'd stressed all day, she had stressed. And yet he'd forgotten?

"I guess it'll have to wait now, but I wanted to get the information for your bank account so I can set up an automatic transfer. That way, money for Sarah-Jane will come to you every month and I won't have to worry about missing a payment."

While she appreciated his commitment, "You couldn't have asked me that over the phone?"

"I didn't think you'd want to put that kind information in a text."

"No, but you could have called." Unless he was one of those people who hated talking on the phone.

"Actually, in this world of identity theft and cybersecurity, I thought you might prefer to type in the info yourself. That's why I had my laptop at the café."

She could see his point, but still. "This is exactly why texting isn't necessarily the best means of communication. If you'd have just called and told me all of that, you could have saved me a lot of worry."

His brow creased. "Why were you worried?"

"Because I thought—" Thankfully she caught herself before revealing the truth—that she was afraid he'd reject Sarah-Jane the way her father had rejected her. "I just was, that's all." They pulled up to her house then, and she hopped out before he could question her any further.

Unfortunately, he followed her. Never mind that they'd spent almost the whole day together. Not that it was Laurel he wanted to be with. He wanted to see Sarah-Jane.

She gave herself a stern shake. She was getting cranky. And after all Wes had done, he didn't deserve to be the object of her ire.

However, the moment she stepped through the back door and saw Sarah-Jane crawling toward her, her spirits lifted.

"There's my girl." Lifting her daughter to her, she kissed her cheek. "I missed you so much."

"Laurel?"

She turned to see Wes standing in front of the kitchen sink.

"You might want to wash up first."

"Ew, yes, you're right." She held Sarah-Jane at arm's length. "Here, Rae. There's no telling what could be all over me."

Rae took hold of the child. "Were you able to accomplish much?"

Laurel had contacted Rae earlier in the day, letting her know the initial assessment. "I think so." She smiled at Sarah-Jane. "I'll be right back, baby." She joined Wes at the sink, his nearness making it difficult to think. He smelled like hard work and peaches, so she was grateful when he started filling his sister in.

"I was impressed at how many people volunteered to help." He soaped up his hands before scrubbing his forearms, a move Laurel mimicked over the adjoining bowl. "Not just to pitch in and help with the grunt work, but to bring food, bottled water, shop vacs. I've not seen that kind of generosity outside of the military."

"Only one of the reasons we love Bliss so much, right, Laurel?"

"You know it, Rae." She scrubbed her fingernails. "But even I was surprised. And I'm glad Wes was there. Especially when Mason Krebbs showed up."

"Looking for business, no doubt." Rae stood near the table now. "He's such a creep."

Wes shook the excess water off his hands before reaching for a towel. "I don't care for people who try to take advantage of others' misfortune."

Laurel ran her arm under the faucet to remove the soap. "It was obvious that Wes was far more knowledgeable than Mason." Yet he didn't demean Mason.

Wes simply stated the facts, even when he had a bad feeling about the guy.

"That's because Wes has built more things in more places than Mason could even imagine."

Laurel accepted the towel from Wes and quickly wiped her hands. "Now where's that baby?"

A smiling Sarah-Jane practically threw herself into Laurel's arms. Yet as Wes took a seat in one of the four dining chairs, her daughter squirmed to get down.

"Okay, fine." No sooner had she set Sarah-Jane on the floor than she took off toward Wes and pulled up on his legs.

"Well, hello there." He picked her up, his face lighting with amusement.

That left Laurel in a quandary. She'd always regretted not having a father and hated that Sarah-Jane was facing that same fate. But seeing her little girl in Wes's arms brought out Laurel's instinct to protect. Could Wes be trusted? Sure, he was Rae's brother, not to mention former military…

"Shall we go play?" Still holding her daughter, Wes stood and went into the living room where Sarah-Jane's toys were.

Okay, so Laurel wasn't concerned about her daughter's physical safety, but there were plenty of other things to worry about. Such as betrayal. What if Wes decided he didn't want to be involved in his daughter's life? Simply paying child support did not make someone a parent. What if he walked away like Laurel's father had? Did she even want him around Sarah-Jane until she had the answers to those questions?

Rae nudged her elbow and pointed to Wes and Sarah-Jane. "I think that's about the sweetest thing I've ever seen."

Wes lay on the floor, grinning at Sarah-Jane, while she sat atop his belly, laughing as though she'd conquered a mountain.

The sight was, indeed, heartwarming, and one Laurel had longed for all her life. Yet from where she stood now, it was also one of the scariest.

"Two weeks?" Phone pressed against his ear just after nine the next morning, Wes paced Irma's front porch, his frustration mounting. It had been bad enough that the other four pest-control companies he'd contacted had said a week to ten days. But two weeks? He didn't have that kind of time. Yet even after he'd explained the situation, they all acted as though coming to Bliss was the equivalent of going to another country. "Sorry, that's not going to work. Thank you."

Ending the call, he dropped into one of two rocking chairs that had been relegated to a corner because of the bathtub. He'd made a commitment to Irma, but now it didn't look as though he'd be able to see it through. He couldn't add the new floor joists until the remaining wood had been treated for termites. And without those joists, everything else was at a standstill, which left him with just a little more than a week to do the remainder of the work. Even if he managed to get some of the downstairs squared away beforehand, he still wasn't likely to finish the job.

Not that he considered it a job. On the contrary, he'd been in his element yesterday as he, Laurel and the folks from church worked to empty Irma's house. Serving others was what Wes was created to do, and it felt good to be working with a purpose again. And that was precisely why he'd signed on with Servant's Heart to go to Iraq. Working simply for a paycheck didn't really suit him, but knowing that he was helping someone, making a difference in their lives… That's what drove him.

Except now it looked as though he wasn't going to be able to help Irma, after all. And if he didn't, who would? Sure, Mason would probably be more than willing to swoop in and do the job, but at what cost to Irma?

With a sigh, Wes slumped back in the chair and watched a pair of cardinals making their way around the sun-speckled front yard, flitting from one tree or bush to another in search of twigs and other nest-building materials. *Lord, did I misunderstand You? All that prompting yesterday. The rationalizing.* Perhaps Wes wasn't supposed to be the one to help Irma.

The sound of a vehicle pulled him from his thoughts, and he looked up to see Laurel's SUV easing alongside the curb. He might as well tell her the bad news. Perhaps she would know of someone other than Mason who could take over.

After exiting her vehicle, she started up the walk. Her hair was pulled back in a long ponytail, and she looked ready to work in a pair of faded jeans and a Dallas Cowboys T-shirt. A moment later, she spotted him, and her gaze instantly narrowed.

Strange to think that two years ago, Laurel had trusted him and they'd connected as though they'd known each other for years. But last night, when he was playing with Sarah-Jane, he'd seen nothing but distrust in her eyes. Then again, he couldn't say that he blamed her. They were, for the most part, strangers. And she had Sarah-Jane to think about. He'd hoped to prove her wrong, to win at least a morsel of her trust. However, this latest development hadn't done him any favors.

"What's wrong?" She moved slowly up the steps.

"I've hit a snag."

Her eyes went wide. "What? Did something else happen inside the house?" She took a step toward the door.

"The house is fine," he said. "Well, not *fine*, but unchanged." He rested his hands on his hips. "It looks as though I'm not going to be able to do the work for Irma after all."

Her gray-green gaze searched his. "Why? What's the problem?"

He blew out a sigh. "I've called five pest-control companies, and the earliest any of them can get out here is late next week. And, unfortunately, any work on that bathroom hinges on getting the remaining wood treated for termites."

"Who all have you called?"

He listed the names, her face contorting more with each one.

"Why would you call them?" She looked at him as though he'd lost his mind.

"Because that's what came up when I did a search for pest control in Bliss, Texas."

"I thought finding a termite person was something you wanted me to help you with. Those folks may be *near* Bliss, but they're not *in* Bliss." She pulled her phone from her back pocket. "You need to call Frank Wurzbach."

"Who's he?"

She looked intently at her phone. "Town councilman, who also happens to own Wurzbach Pest Control."

"I saw the name in my search, but they didn't have a website, so I skipped it. Is he any good?"

Glancing up at him, she frowned. "Wes, Bliss may be small, and a lot of people are old-school, but don't be so quick to discount them. What we lack in quantity, we make up for in quality." Sounded like something his sister would have said.

"Do you have his number?"

Laurel again focused on her phone. "I've got it here somewhere." A couple of finger taps later, she said, "There. I just sent it to you." She tucked her phone away as his vibrated in his hand.

"Thanks."

"Be sure to tell Frank you're working on Irma's house. I guarantee that'll get him out here right away."

"Well, we need to let the wood dry over the weekend, but that's good to know." He logged the number into his contacts. "So, what are you doing here?"

She poked a thumb over her shoulder in the general direction of the front door. "I need to check on those books and other things the ladies and I set out to dry last night."

"Where's Sarah-Jane?"

"Irma and Joyce are watching her."

The thought of two elderly ladies caring for an active infant who happened to be his daughter made him uneasy. "Where?"

"At Joyce's house."

"Wouldn't it have been better for them to come to your place?"

"Perhaps. But I didn't want to inconvenience them. Besides, Joyce has a little dog, and Sarah-Jane loves dogs."

Maybe so, but some dogs weren't too fond of little kids. "Do you think she'll be okay with them?"

"Why wouldn't she be?" Exasperation wove its way through her words. "The two of them will probably dote on her so much she might never want to come home. And just for the record, if I thought she was in any danger, I wouldn't have taken her over there in the first place."

"But what if Sarah-Jane wears them out?"

"Then I guess they won't offer again, will they?" Nostrils flared, she turned and pushed through the front door, where the roar of the air movers drowned out everything else.

That didn't stop him, though. He followed her into the parlor, the smell of old house circling around him as he stepped in front of her. "Why are you so upset with me?" He had to raise his voice to be heard over the incessant rumble. "You act as though it's a crime for me to be concerned about my daughter."

"I have no problem with your concern for Sarah-Jane," she countered. "But what I don't appreciate is you coming in here and questioning my judgment. I've been taking care of Sarah-Jane since the day she was born—quite well, I might add—with no help from you, thank you very much."

"And whose fault is that?" As soon as the words left Wes's mouth, he wished he could take them back. And the tears that sprang to Laurel's eyes didn't help.

Frustrated, he strode into the entry hall and turned off the blower in there before continuing into the family room and doing the same with the three in there. On his way back, he went into the bedroom and killed the two units that were drying the carpet.

Surrounded by virtual silence, save for the blowers upstairs and the sound of his boots against the wooden floorboards, he crossed to where Laurel still stood, feeling like a major jerk. "I'm sorry. I didn't mean what I said. I know you had no way to get in touch with me. And I shouldn't have pushed you so hard. You're a good mother. I know you would never put Sarah-Jane in any kind of danger."

Arms wrapped tightly around her middle, she nodded without ever looking at him. "We both have work to do." With that, she continued into the dining room, leaving Wes to wonder if he'd just dug himself a hole he might not be able to climb out of.

Chapter Six

The stress of the last two days had finally caught up to Laurel. Wes's sudden appearance had her drifting into uncharted waters. And for a moment today, she'd felt as though she might drown.

She couldn't blame Wes, though, not when she'd thrown the first punch. Yet while he'd been quick to apologize, she had yet to say a word. Even now, as she was ready to leave Irma's, she wasn't sure she could muster the courage to say she was sorry.

Despite the incessant droning of the fans threatening to drive her crazy, her steps halted as she approached the front door just after noon. Wes was on the other side. He'd informed her half an hour ago that he was going out there to make some phone calls. Perhaps he'd be on the phone now, allowing her to simply wave as she escaped to her vehicle.

Unfortunately, when she opened the door, he was standing on the other side.

His blue eyes seemed fixed on her as he stepped aside, allowing her to join him.

"I, uh, I'm going to head out." She somehow managed to move the words past her suddenly tight throat.

"I need to get Sarah-Jane down for a nap." And maybe even grab one herself. Except she had work to catch up on. As a CPA who specialized in working with ex-pats, she prided herself on addressing their needs in a timely manner. And after being out of the office all day yesterday, there were things that required her attention.

"Yeah, I'm going to cut out shortly myself." His voice sounded strained, as though he was uneasy. "By the way, I called Frank, and he'll be out here on Monday."

"Oh, that's good." She nodded repeatedly, probably looking like a bobblehead doll.

"Yeah. So it looks like I'll be able to do the work after all."

"That's great." Actually, it really was, because the busier he stayed, the less time Laurel would have to spend with him.

But what about Sarah-Jane?

"Would, uh, would you mind if I stopped by to see Sarah-Jane later? After her nap."

"I don't know." Conflicted, she shifted from one sneaker-covered foot to the next, watching the leaves on a large oak tree sway in the breeze. "I was really hoping to make it an early night."

"Me, too. Yesterday kind of wore us out. However, I'd still like to see her. I've only got a couple more weeks, and I'd like to use them to get to know my daughter."

Her gaze jerked to his. *My daughter.* He wielded those two words as if they'd gain him access. Not that she would deny her daughter a relationship with her father. But that relationship was still in its infancy, and Laurel wanted to make sure Wes was in it for the long haul before she gave him carte blanche.

"I'll even bring dinner," he added.

All right, now he was playing dirty. Because the

mere thought of planning, let alone preparing, a meal sucked what little life was left right out of her. "What did you have in mind?"

"Rae says there's a burger joint around here that's hard to beat."

Bubba's. Laurel's mouth watered, and her stomach growled just thinking about it. Wes did not play fair.

With a fortifying breath, or, perhaps, one of resignation, she said, "In that case, I'll take a loaded cheeseburger with a large fry and a chocolate milkshake."

"And Sarah-Jane?"

"Chicken nuggets, of course."

His smile was genuine as she strode off the porch, headed for her SUV. "All right, then I'll see you around five thirty?"

"Sounds good." Or at least the meal did, anyway.

When she picked up Sarah-Jane, Irma and Joyce gushed about what a good baby she was and how much they'd enjoyed spending time with her. But Sarah-Jane's good mood was quickly coming to an end. After being up later than her usual eight o'clock bedtime last night, she was more than ready for a nap and fell asleep on the way home.

Over the next two hours, Laurel managed to distract herself with work, emailing a couple of clients and following up on an outstanding case with the IRS. Then, after Sarah-Jane had awoken, the two of them played and Laurel did a load of laundry, all the while pondering the things she'd like to tackle at Irma's. While picking up Sarah-Jane, Laurel had mentioned to Irma that Wes was hoping they could salvage the carpet in the bedroom. However, Irma had quickly told her to instruct him not to bother, because she hated the ugly brown stuff. And that got Laurel to thinking. Maybe there were other cosmetic things that could be done to refresh some of the spaces impacted by the collapse.

Those thoughts seemed to fade away as five thirty drew nearer, though, replaced by a whole lot of angst. How could she spend the evening with Wes with her spiteful words still hanging between them? Conflict was not something she relished. She was an only child, for crying out loud. She'd had no siblings to argue with. Or, more to the point, to make up with. How did she tell Wes she was sorry?

Pride goeth before the fall.

Pride? Was that really her problem?

Only where Wes was concerned.

Laurel prided herself on being a good mother to Sarah-Jane. So, when he'd started questioning her about leaving her daughter with Irma and Joyce, ladies Laurel trusted, she'd lashed out, wanting to discount him the way she thought he was doing to her. Now she was left with the bitter taste of regret. And that was not going to go well with her Bubba burger.

She had just finished changing Sarah-Jane's diaper when someone knocked on the door. Checking her watch, she noted that Wes was right on time. Another trait that had carried over from his military career, no doubt.

"Are you ready for some dinner, baby?" She held Sarah-Jane in one arm while she opened the door with the other.

Wes clutched a white paper bag in one hand and a drink carrier in the other, his face lighting up when he saw Sarah-Jane. "There's my favorite girl." He pressed a kiss to her chubby cheek as he entered. "I hope you two are ready to eat—" he continued into the kitchen

"—because the smells coming from this bag are making my stomach grumble."

Laurel set a wiggling Sarah-Jane on the floor before closing the door. "We sure are."

After setting the food on the rustic wooden table, Wes intercepted a speed-crawling Sarah-Jane at the opening between the living room and dining space. "Let's get you in your high chair."

Laurel watched him slip the child into her seat and carefully strap her in. Like her, all Wes wanted was what was best for Sarah-Jane. How could Laurel fault him for that?

While he finished up, Laurel emptied the contents of the bag onto the table. She popped a fry into her mouth before breaking up another and setting it on Sarah-Jane's tray.

"What about me?" Wes looked at her expectantly. "I think I have some fries in there, too."

Puffing out a laugh, Laurel grabbed another fry and handed it to him.

"Thank you." He popped it into his mouth, his playful gaze never leaving hers, reminding her of the man she'd met two years ago. The one who made her laugh and whose company she truly enjoyed.

With him standing close enough for her to smell the clean aroma of his soap, she stared at her hands. "Earlier today, at Irma's, I said things to you that I shouldn't have." She looked up at him. "I'm sorry. I had no right to accuse you of something you had no control over."

"It's all right. I think tensions were rather high for both of us this morning. I was frustrated, and you were worn out from yesterday."

"You don't have to make excuses for me. I'm big

enough to admit that I was wrong." She lifted a shoulder. "Eventually, anyway."

"If I say you're forgiven, can we eat?"

She shook her head. "No, I'll probably eat regardless."

"Good, because there's nothing to forgive." He pulled out a white chair and sat down beside Sarah-Jane.

Moving to the other side of their daughter, Laurel took a seat, watching the man who seemed to truly want to be a part of his daughter's life. Yet there was one thing she couldn't seem to forget.

Wes believes he doesn't deserve a family.

For now, he seemed to have forgotten that. But what would happen when he remembered the lie that haunted him for much of his life? And how would the fallout impact Sarah-Jane?

Wes stood atop a new, much more stable ladder in Irma's family room Friday morning, peering into the gaping hole overhead and evaluating the joists—partial joists, in some cases—that remained. Anything that wasn't sound, he cut away, leaving the rest to be treated.

Reciprocating saw in hand, he trimmed another section, his mind drifting back to last night. Who knew babies could be so therapeutic? Certainly not him. Of course, he'd never really been around babies before. Yet having a chance to spend time with Sarah-Jane had been exactly what he needed to vanquish the stress of the past couple days. And he was surprised by the feelings she stirred inside him. They were unlike anything he'd ever felt before. She was his own flesh and blood—a hefty concept that sparked all sorts of unfamiliar instincts.

Even Laurel had seemed to enjoy herself, at least for a short time, reminding him of the woman who'd lived in his mind for the past two years and making him wonder what might have happened had he known about Sarah-Jane from the beginning. Would he have tried to explore a relationship with Laurel? With them living in two different states, it wouldn't have been easy. Not to mention his vow to never have a family. His bad choices had killed his parents and changed Laurel's life forever. He couldn't risk hurting someone again.

Still, there was no way he would have turned his back on his own child.

He wanted to be a part of her life. How would he do that, though, when he'd be living on the other side of the world for the next year? And what about when he came back? To be a real father, he'd need to live close enough to see Sarah-Jane every day. Could he make a home in Bliss? And how would Laurel feel about that?

He couldn't worry about that now. He needed to get things squared away here before he headed back to Rae's to help her with some painting. With both of them pitching in, they might be able to get the bulk of it done tonight. And while it would mean time away from Sarah-Jane, at least it would free him up for the weekend. With Irma's home still in the drying process, he was hoping to do something fun with Laurel and Sarah-Jane.

"Wes?"

He barely heard his name over the roar of the blowers that had been running around the clock since Wednesday.

"Family room," he hollered before making his way down the ladder.

"Hey." Though Laurel smiled as she entered the empty space, there was a hesitance about her. Moving beside him, she said, "I need to talk to you about something."

Nodding, he held up a finger to indicate he needed a moment. After setting the saw on the tarp he'd laid down to catch the rotted wood and protect the floor, he turned off the air movers in the family room and hall. Since he'd already turned off the upstairs units to keep wood from flying everywhere, things were almost silent, except for the distant sound of the two in the bedroom down the hall.

"You were saying?"

"I've been thinking, as long as we're having to do all this work—" she motioned around the room "—what if we also refreshed things a little bit?"

Having worked with several hard-to-please homeowners since leaving the military, he couldn't help wondering just how little a little bit meant. "What did you have in mind?"

"Mostly cosmetic stuff. Maybe repaint this space and her bedroom, since those two rooms are where she spends most of her time."

"That's easy enough."

"Oh, and Irma said for you to go ahead and deep-six the carpeting in her bedroom. Apparently her late husband picked it out and had it installed to surprise her." Laurel giggled, and he couldn't help thinking how cute she sounded. "She said she was surprised, all right, but not in a good way. However, she didn't have the heart to tell him, so she's lived with 'ugly brown'—" she did air quotes with her fingers "—ever since."

"How long were they married?"

"Fifty years."

"After all that time, you'd think he'd have had enough sense to consult with her first."

"You would think." She motioned for him to follow her before starting down the hall.

He did so, detouring into the bedroom to kill the blowers in there before joining her in the parlor. For the umpteenth time, he eyed the stacks of boxes that covered a third of the space. "I can't believe all of this came out of her bedroom." His gaze drifted to Laurel. "This could border on hoarding, you know."

"Hardly." She flipped open one and pulled out a stack of photos. "These are memories, Wes." She waved them as if to emphasize her point. "High school yearbooks, baby books, baby clothes… I even found Irma's wedding dress." She pointed to a stack of boxes nearest to her. "Every one of these is filled with photographs. Her parents, her kids, wedding photos. And to Irma's credit, every single picture is labeled." Laurel shook her head. "I sure wish Grandmama had done that. I can't tell you how many pictures I tossed because I had no clue who the people were."

"But what good is all this stuff if it just lives in a box?"

"Exactly! That's why I've been doing so much digging. I thought that, maybe, when we put things back together, some of these things could be displayed."

"Even the wedding dress?"

"Maybe, if I could get my hands on a dress form." She touched a finger to her lips. "Hmm, I wonder if Drenda might have one of those at her shop?"

"You know I was kidding, right?"

"Yes, but it's still a great idea."

Leaning against the bookshelf that had been moved from the family room, he couldn't help admiring her enthusiasm. "Do you take many pictures?"

"Ha! You have no idea. My phone alone is an album of Sarah-Jane's entire life."

He straightened then. "Can I see them?"

She looked up from a box, blinking. "I guess you would be curious about that, wouldn't you?"

"I may not have been here to experience her first fourteen months—" he moved closer "—but I could live vicariously."

"All right. Then I guess we should start from the beginning." She pulled her phone from the back pocket of her shorts, and a few finger taps later, he was looking at a black-and-white image of a bean. "This was the very first time I saw her. It was taken at my first OB appointment." She pointed to the bean. "That's Sarah-Jane right there."

Her enthusiasm was contagious. Yet as he watched this strong, independent woman, he couldn't help realizing how difficult that moment must have been. She was pregnant by someone who not only wasn't in the picture but was, for all intents and purposes, a stranger. "Were you scared?"

"Yes. But thinking of that little life growing inside me made me unbelievably happy."

"I wish I could have been there to share it with you. To help you."

She lifted a shoulder. "We can't change the past, Wes."

He was probably more aware of that than she knew. Still— "No, but the future is up for grabs. And I'd like to be a part of Sarah-Jane's future. I want to teach her how to ride a bike and be the one who puts the bandage on her knee when she falls off."

"Wait, you're planning to let our daughter fall?"

He grinned. "I want to be there to see her off on her

first date. Of course, that won't happen until she's at least thirty-one." He laughed. "And to see her graduate from high school, college… I want to walk her down the aisle when she gets married."

Laurel held up a hand, cutting him off. "Okay, stop. I am *so* not ready to think that far ahead. She's not even walking yet."

"Well, maybe she'll do that while I'm here. And it can be the first of many firsts."

As she watched him, there was an uncertainty in her eyes. "I guess we'll just have to wait and see."

Chapter Seven

He wanted to give Sarah-Jane away at her wedding?

Almost twenty-four hours later, Laurel still couldn't believe Wes had actually said that. Not only was she nowhere near ready to think about Sarah-Jane getting married, but who was to say Wes would even be around then? Sure, it might sound nice now, but he was about to leave for a year. A lot could change in twelve months. He might decide he didn't want to come back to Bliss. That he didn't want to be a father.

But what if he does?

She didn't want to think about that, either. She and Sarah-Jane had plans this morning, and they didn't include Wes. For all she knew, he was still busy painting at Rae's. Yesterday, that had afforded Laurel her first night without him since he learned about Sarah-Jane four days ago. And while she appreciated his commitment, no matter how short-lived it could potentially be, she also liked having a relaxing evening to herself. Because, let's face it, having someone who could impact the life of your child around was stressful. And she'd had more than enough stress for one week.

With the midmorning sun filtering through the oak

tree in her front yard, she blew out a frustrated breath and settled Sarah-Jane into her stroller. "Want to go to the farmers market? Maybe they'll still have some dewberries so Mommy can make another cobbler."

Not that she needed another cobbler, especially since she'd just polished off the last of Irma's chocolate cake. But Grandmama's dewberry cobbler was her favorite and brought back such fond memories.

Stooping to fasten the straps around Sarah-Jane, Laurel pondered the woman who'd been the one constant throughout her life. Actually, Laurel had her to thank for ending up in Bliss. Having inherited her grandmother's house in Dallas and a decent life insurance policy, Laurel had finally been able to leave her corporate job and branch out on her own. Then she'd found out she was pregnant. And while Dallas was a nice place to live, Laurel wanted a different kind of life for her child. A simpler life.

She straightened, admiring her sweet slate blue house with the inviting front porch. Thanks to her grandmother, she'd found that life in Bliss. Though with the appearance of Wes, things had definitely gotten more complicated.

Shoving the thought aside, she started along the sidewalk, savoring the blissful weather this last Saturday of April had brought. Neither she nor Sarah-Jane needed a jacket. The sun was bright, the temperature not too hot and not too cold, which made their journey to the courthouse square beyond pleasurable. If only every day could be like this. Of course, then she'd never get any work done, because it would be sheer torture to stay cooped up inside.

Ten minutes later, they arrived at the square where people were selling farm-fresh eggs, baked goods, plants, produce and, yes, dewberries. Well aware that the season was coming to an end, Laurel decided to buy an extra bag to freeze. That way, she could enjoy her favorite cobbler later in the year.

"How much do I owe you?" In the shade of a magnificent old live oak that dripped with Spanish moss and swayed with the gentle breeze, Laurel eyed the blonde on the other side of the table.

"I've got it."

She turned as Wes passed a twenty to the lady.

"I love blackberries," he said.

"Those aren't blackberries," Laurel informed him. "They're dewberries. And I can pay for them myself." She stretched a hand with her own twenty toward the woman, nudging Wes's out of the way.

Though he withdrew his money, he didn't look happy about it. "I don't think I've ever heard of dewberries before."

"Probably because you're not from Texas. They grow wild." She held the bag open. "Go ahead. Try one." Watching as he grabbed one, she tried not to laugh. Dewberries might look like blackberries, but they were quite tart.

He popped a couple in his mouth and promptly puckered. "Ooh, those are sour."

"Just a little. But they make a great cobbler."

"Wait, you cook?"

"On occasion." She closed the bag. "Depends on the motivation."

"And you're motivated by cobbler?"

"Dewberry cobbler, yes. Don't worry, it has plenty of sugar."

Laurel accepted her change while Wes crouched beside the stroller.

"I missed seeing you yesterday, sweetheart."

A smiling Sarah-Jane offered him a bite of her graham cracker, which he pretended to nibble.

"It's a beautiful day." Standing, he faced Laurel again. "What do you say we all go do something?"

And give her another opportunity to get a glimpse of how wonderful he could be. The way she had the other night at dinner, when she'd carelessly let her guard down. "Like what?"

"I don't know. Something Sarah-Jane would enjoy."

She'd already been contemplating taking Sarah-Jane to Founder's Knoll. Not only did it have a beautiful view overlooking the river, between the nature trails and the playground, there was plenty to keep Sarah-Jane entertained. Except, when the thought had popped into Laurel's head, Wes hadn't been part of the equation. But now that he was here and being rather insistent, she supposed an extra set of eyes would be beneficial.

Depositing the berries and her wallet in the basket beneath the stroller, she said, "I have an idea. It's not far, but we'll need to drive."

"My truck is right there." He pointed toward the café on the other side of the street.

"You don't have a car seat, though. Besides, I'll need to grab the diaper bag and some snacks for Sarah-Jane."

Wes accompanied them back to their place, and a little more than an hour later, they were strolling along a wide dirt trail bordered with lush green foliage.

"This is amazing." Wes gazed at the expansive oak canopy.

Hands shoved in the pockets of her jeans, Laurel breathed in the fresh air, hoping for a calm she hadn't had since Wes showed up at the square. "Founder's Knoll is one of Bliss's most overlooked treasures."

"I guess that's both good and bad." He turned his attention to Laurel. "Good for us because it's not crowded, but bad for those who've missed out on something so beautiful."

"This is nice, but wait until we reach the top."

"Well, that's intrig—" His eyes suddenly lit up, and he knelt to the ground. He looked as though he was picking up something.

So long as it wasn't a snake.

"Look, Sarah-Jane." Moving in front of the stroller, he lowered his hand. "It's a little lizard." He held the tiny creature between his finger and thumb as Sarah-Jane looked on in wonder.

Laurel pulled her phone from her pocket and snapped a picture. "What do you think about that, baby?"

Her daughter reached out a finger to touch it, grinning when it flicked its tail.

"Be gentle." Wes's voice was tender, and Laurel was impressed that her daughter actually seemed to understand, slowing her movements.

"That's right." Wes smiled as she carefully touched the creature. "Okay, we have to let him go now." He set it on the ground, and Sarah-Jane leaned over to watch the lizard scurry off into the ground cover.

As they continued on, Wes turned his attention to Laurel. "Does having me around bother you? I mean, things were so easy between us in Vegas. Now you seem…tense."

Last week at this time she'd been just fine, but now… "I'm the same person I've always been, but I'm a mother now, and I have to protect Sarah-Jane."

"You think I pose a threat to her?"

Laurel's steps slowed as they came to the open area atop the bluff that overlooked the river and the rolling hills that surrounded Bliss. She might not like conflict, but all of this tiptoeing around, torn between wanting Sarah-Jane to know her father and fearing he'd eventually reject her the way Laurel's father had done with her, was eating her up. She needed to just get everything out in the open.

"Well, you are leaving soon."

He squinted against the sun. "But I'll be back."

"Will you?" She continued toward a picnic table situated beneath a tree and forced herself to look at him. "A lot could change in a year, Wes."

"I can't believe this. You act as though I don't want to be with her."

Laurel opened her mouth to argue, but he continued.

"Have you ever stopped to think that, maybe, you're not the only one who's worried? I mean, here I am, suddenly in her life, yet in two weeks, I'll be gone. How is that going to impact her? And what about when I come back? Will she even remember me? Will she wonder where I've been and if I'm going to leave again?" He rubbed the back of his neck. "I don't want to mess with her or have her grow up thinking her father doesn't want to be with her—because I do. More than anything. And if I wasn't already committed to going to Iraq, I wouldn't leave at all. Unfortunately, I am committed. So, tell me what I should do, Laurel, because I don't want to do something that's going to hurt my daughter in the long run."

Laurel just stood there, blinking up at him. He really had looked at the big picture. And not just the good parts, like walking Sarah-Jane down the aisle. He'd actually considered the effects of his actions.

She swallowed hard, her heart twisting. How was it

possible to go from feeling skeptical to being completely enamored with someone in the span of thirty seconds?

Easy. Wes loves his daughter.

And that had melted her heart faster than butter in the Texas summer sun.

Reluctant to allow her mind to go down that path, she drew in a deep breath and willed her pulse back to a normal rate. "You know, technology is a wonderful thing. Even though you'll be half a world away, you and Sarah-Jane will still be able to see each other via video calls. I assume you'll have internet."

"Yes. Though I'm not sure to what extent."

"Then there you go. I Skype with my clients all the time. So it won't be as though you're disappearing from her life."

He ran his fingers over the stubble that lined his chin. "I hadn't thought of that." A smile lifted the corners of his mouth, erasing the lines that had creased his forehead as he knelt beside his daughter and reached for her hand. "Technology isn't necessarily my forte, but I'm willing to learn. Because being able to see each other would certainly make our time apart easier." His eyes never left his daughter. "And I can continue to see her while I'm here." He hesitated then. Standing again, he looked at Laurel. "If that's okay with you."

Her daughter was being granted the one thing Laurel had always wanted—a father who loved her and wanted to be with her. So what else could she say?

"Fine by me." However, given the sudden condition of her heart, his leaving might end up being harder on her than she ever imagined.

Wes felt better knowing that he and Sarah-Jane would still be able to see each other while he was in

Iraq. Even if it was on a computer screen, that was better than nothing. What he couldn't understand, though, was why Laurel would think he wasn't coming back when his year was up. Granted, living in Bliss, Texas, had never blipped on his radar before, but then, he'd never planned to have children, either. However, now that he knew about Sarah-Jane, wild horses couldn't keep him away.

Why would Laurel question that? Even if he still couldn't see himself with a wife and kids, what's done was done. He wouldn't turn his back on his daughter. He'd just have to accept that God had a different plan for his life and then try to be the best father Sarah-Jane could ask for.

In the parking lot of Bliss's lone grocery store, he loaded plastic bags into the back seat of his truck, suddenly curious about Laurel's father. While he'd heard her mention her mother and grandmother before, there hadn't been a word about her father. And since it had been Laurel's grandmother who had raised her after her mother died, Wes couldn't help wondering what the story was with her father.

Sarah-Jane and I have done just fine without you.

He closed the door, recalling the determination in Laurel's voice that night Wes had tried to explain his trepidation over being Sarah-Jane's father. Could the absence of her father have been why Laurel had reacted so strongly?

The only way Wes would ever know was to ask her. Yet while they'd been honest with each other regarding their individual concerns about his future with Sarah-Jane this afternoon, asking Laurel about her father could threaten their fragile friendship.

With his groceries loaded, he climbed behind the

wheel and headed back to Laurel's. After a couple of hours at Founder's Knoll, Sarah-Jane had become grumpy. The kind of grumpy no amount of snacks could appease, a good indicator that she was ready for a nap, according to Laurel. After returning to her place, Wes discovered a great backyard complete with a deck and grill. Considering what a beautiful day it had been, he offered to grill some steaks for dinner and was pleased when Laurel not only said yes, but that it gave her an excuse to make that dewberry cobbler she'd talked about. He was curious to try it, despite his less-than-favorable opinion of the fruit.

So, while Sarah-Jane napped, Laurel called Rae to invite her to join them, and Wes headed to the store for rib-eye steaks, potatoes for baking, salad and some vanilla ice cream to go with the cobbler. Now, as he returned to Laurel's, he hoped he could find a way to get her to open up about her father—without her shutting down or ending up mad at him.

Lord, You've granted me a precious gift in the form of Sarah-Jane. Please don't let me do or say anything that might hurt her mother.

"These are some nice-looking steaks," Laurel said as she removed them from the bag in her kitchen a short time later. "What type of seasoning do you use?" She opened the stainless steel refrigerator and set them inside.

"A little bit of salt, some pepper and a touch of garlic powder." He set the large baking potatoes on the marble counter. "Just enough to bring out the flavor of the meat, not cover it up."

Smiling, she rested her hip against the counter, watching him as he unloaded sour cream, cheese and bacon bits for the potatoes. "Sounds like you've done this a time or two."

"What can I say? I appreciate a good steak."

"I'm sure the cattle ranchers of Bliss will thank you for that." A slight noise drew her attention to the video monitor sitting on the opposite counter.

He turned toward the small screen, watching his daughter rouse from her slumber. "That's a pretty cool gadget you've got there."

"I know, I love it. Saves me from having to guess what she's doing in there or disturbing her by trying to sneak a peek." As she spoke, Sarah-Jane moved to her knees, then pulled up on the side of the crib. "Guess I'd better go get her."

He gathered up the items that needed to go into the fridge. "I'll be checking on the grill to see if it needs to be cleaned. When was the last time you used it?"

Her face contorted as she thought. "New Year's Eve, when Rae, Christa, Paisley and I rang in the new year."

"Sounds like fun."

"It was." Smiling, she headed down the hall.

After depositing the items in the refrigerator, he made his way onto the wooden deck that overlooked a decent-size backyard with a lush lawn. A couple of well-established trees sat near the back of the property, their deep green leaves dancing in the slightest of breezes. Man, it was a beautiful day. One you wanted to set on repeat to play over and over.

A sweet fragrance touched his nose then, drawing his attention to the wisteria-covered fence on the other side of the driveway. The vines dripped with clusters of purple flowers in a spectacular show of color.

Lifting the lid on the gas grill, he noticed the wire brush dangling from a hook. One glance at the grates told him he was definitely going to need that. He'd just started scrubbing when the back door opened, and Laurel emerged holding Sarah-Jane.

"Somebody's in a very good mood." A smile lit Laurel's gray-green eyes as she stood the child in front of her, keeping hold of her hand.

Wes knelt opposite his daughter. "Did you have a good nap, Sarah-Jane?"

She smiled and bounced. Seconds later, she let go of Laurel's finger and took a step.

Laurel's quick intake of air was hard to miss as she watched her little girl.

Still kneeling, Wes stretched his hands toward Sarah-Jane. "Come on, sweetheart, you can do it."

She stepped once more, then bobbled, but caught herself before continuing. Several steps later, she collapsed into Wes's waiting arms.

"You did it, Sarah-Jane!" He hugged her tight, pride weaving through him.

"I can't believe it." Laurel pressed a hand to her cheek. "That's more steps than she's ever taken. She was actually walking all by herself."

"I guess you just had to strengthen up those legs, didn't you, Sarah-Jane?" Still holding his daughter, he stood.

"Or have the right motivation."

He looked at Laurel to find her smiling as she approached.

She took hold of her daughter's hand. "Were you showing off for your daddy?" Laurel froze then and so did he.

Their eyes met.

"I—I'm sorry." She took a step back. "That just kind of slipped out."

"No, it's okay." He smoothed a hand over his daughter's back. "Daddy is a distinction I will wear proudly." But could Laurel say the same about her father?

She started to turn away.

"Laurel?"

"Yes?" She faced him again.

Suddenly he was nervous. This wonderful moment could be blown to smithereens if he put his foot in his mouth again.

Lord, help me get this right.

"You've told me a little bit about your mother and your grandmother. But what about your father?"

Her eyes seemed to search his before falling to the weathered boards beneath their feet. And when she wrapped her arms around herself, he wished he hadn't brought it up.

"That's okay, you don't have to—"

"He went to jail when I was a little younger than Sarah-Jane." She rubbed her arms now. "It was only supposed to be for six months, but he didn't come back for us. My mom and I, we never saw him again."

He didn't come back for us. Those six words hit him like a ton of bricks. No wonder she had such concerns about Wes leaving. She was convinced he was going to do the same thing. Leave and never come back for Sarah-Jane.

In two steps, he closed the distance between them, determined to make her understand that he was not like her father. "Laurel, I'm sorry. I shouldn't have pried like that."

"It's fine, Wes. You weren't prying."

He looked at the child he still held in his arms. "I promise you right here and now, unless the good Lord decides to take me home, I will be back. Sarah-Jane is my daughter. And while the role of father may be one I was hesitant to take on, I would never turn my back on my own flesh and blood. The love I feel for her is something I still can't fathom, but it's there and it's strong and it's more real than anything I've ever felt before."

Lips pursed, she smiled, nodding repeatedly. She didn't believe him. And, unfortunately, it would be a year before he could prove himself, which meant he'd have to work all the harder now to convince her that he was a man of his word. But that was proving to be more difficult with each and every day, because keeping his word to Servant's Heart meant stepping away from the most important role of his life. And that might prove to be the most difficult thing he'd ever done.

Chapter Eight

For the life of her, Laurel couldn't figure out why she'd told Wes about her father. That was so not like her to open up to someone she barely knew, yet she seemed to do it over and over—first in Vegas, and then yesterday. Just because he'd asked about her father didn't mean she had to tell him. But did that stop her? Not one bit.

The love I feel for her is something I still can't fathom, but it's there and it's strong and it's more real than anything I've ever felt before.

Even now as she sat in the sanctuary of Bliss Community Church, those words brought tears to her eyes. And while they could be just that—words—the depth of sincerity in Wes's voice and his expression had told her that Sarah-Jane was one blessed little girl. A little girl who was now walking. Laurel still couldn't believe it.

If only she hadn't referred to Wes as *daddy.* Even though it may be true, there was something about saying it out loud that had felt rather intimate, like a term of endearment shared between a couple. Something she and Wes definitely were not. Instead, they were barely friends. Not that there weren't times when she wondered what it might be like if they were more.

Like right now as she sat in the pew, wedged between him and Rae during Sunday morning worship service.

She surreptitiously glanced his way, taking in the sound of his baritone voice as he sang, the scent of soap and raw masculinity, and the blue plaid shirt that matched his eyes… To top it all off, the man was oblivious to how attractive he really was, which made him even more appealing. Yet while she'd admittedly allowed herself to fall for him once, she couldn't afford to do it again. Not when it meant she could get hurt. While Wes might be accepting of his daughter, Laurel and Sarah-Jane weren't a package deal. And if her parents had taught her anything, it was that Laurel was disposable.

"I like that pastor." Wes followed Laurel and Rae out of the sanctuary after the service and into the long hallway that led to classrooms and the fellowship hall. "He's not all flowery and doesn't try to impress everyone with his knowledge. He just tells it like it is."

Even though Laurel's mind had been too preoccupied to listen to the sermon, she agreed wholeheartedly. Bliss Community was not the first church she'd visited when she arrived, but it was where she'd felt at home.

"One of many reasons we will do whatever is needed to keep Pastor Kleinschmidt around," said Rae.

"Rae!"

All three of them turned to see Anita McWhorter hurrying to catch up. The woman in her midforties with short sandy-colored hair pulled some papers from her Bible. "Here's that information I promised you about becoming a foster parent."

Rae, who was in her early forties and had never had children, smiled as she accepted the papers. "Oh, good.

I've got a couple of questions I'd like to ask you, though. Have you got a minute?"

"Sure."

Rae glanced at Wes and Laurel. "You two grab Sarah-Jane. I'll catch up."

Wes leaned toward Laurel as they again moved down the hallway. "Foster parent?"

"Yes. There's a huge need right now." Something that always broke Laurel's heart. If she didn't legally name a guardian for Sarah-Jane and something happened to Laurel, her daughter would be one of those kids. Unfortunately, between the accident and Wes's sudden appearance, she had yet to take action.

"But why would Rae want to do that?"

Stopping, Laurel looked up at him curiously. "Because she loves kids. She's a born nurturer, and since she never had any children of her own..."

He glanced back at his sister with a fondness Laurel hadn't seen before. "Rae is definitely a nurturer. Yet that louse of a husband she had never wanted kids." His gaze shifted to Laurel. "At least, not with her."

That was obviously a reference to the fact that Rae's ex had married his pregnant mistress and then gone on to father two more children with her.

"Well, from what I've been able to gather," said Laurel, "she's better off without him."

"That's for sure." The corners of Wes's mouth tipped upward as they started walking again. "I guess this foster thing is why she's so eager to get her apartment fixed up."

"Probably."

The sounds of children at play drifted into the hall as they approached the nursery. One of the workers was holding Sarah-Jane when they stopped outside the brightly colored room. As always, Sarah-Jane's smile was wide as she reached for Laurel.

"Here's her diaper bag." The worker passed it over the half door.

"I can take that." Wes reached for the backpack.

"Say goodbye, Sarah-Jane." Laurel encouraged the child to wave, but Sarah-Jane wasn't having any part of it.

With a final farewell, Laurel again started down the hallway and almost bumped into Pastor Kleinschmidt. "I'm so sorry."

"No, no, you're the one with the baby," said the pastor. "I simply wasn't watching where I was going." The balding man in his late fifties turned his attention to Wes. "I don't believe we've met. I'm Ron Kleinschmidt."

"Where are my manners?" Laurel looked from one man to the next. "Pastor, this is Wes Bishop. He's—" She saw the way the pastor's eyes shifted from Wes to Sarah-Jane. Was this the right time to introduce Wes as Sarah-Jane's father? After all, Bliss was a small town. And while the pastor may not talk, if anyone else overheard… "—Rae's brother."

"Oh yes." The pastor shook Wes's hand. "Rae told me you were going to be in town for a few weeks. I also hear you're taking care of the repairs over at Irma's."

"Yes, sir." Wes looked from the pastor to her. "Though it's Laurel who's calling the shots."

Pastor Kleinschmidt's gaze homed in on Wes. "Rae mentioned that you'd accepted a job with a mission organization in Iraq."

"Servant's Heart, yes. I'll be working on some rebuilding projects." He slung Sarah-Jane's pack over one shoulder. "Having served over there, it'll be nice to aid the Iraqi people in a less intimidating capacity."

"Well, the church will certainly keep you in our prayers."

"Thank you. I'd appreciate that, sir."

Sarah-Jane chose that moment to start fussing. She rubbed her eyes.

"Looks like I'm not the only one who's ready for a nap." The pastor patted the child on the back.

"Probably." Laurel finger combed her daughter's hair to one side. "She had a lot of excitement yesterday." Her gaze inadvertently drifted to Wes. "She took her first steps."

"Uh-oh." The pastor's expression turned serious. "If you thought you were busy before…"

"Trust me, I've already thought about that." She shifted her daughter to the other arm. "Come on, sweet pea. Let's get you home."

"It was nice to meet you, Wes." The pastor waved as they walked away.

Wes held the door for Laurel as they continued outside.

"Thank you." A bird's song carried on the gentle breeze as she stepped into the midday warmth. The weather was almost a carbon copy of yesterday's, though perhaps with just a tad more humidity.

Stopping, Wes faced her, his expression suddenly serious. "So, is that how it's going to be, Laurel? I'm Sarah-Jane's daddy behind closed doors, but in public I'm Rae's brother?"

Laurel's whole being cringed as she recognized the hurt etched across his handsome face. While he'd been there to witness Sarah-Jane's first steps, he hadn't been able to share the joy when Laurel had talked about it because she'd been too busy worrying what someone else might think. Why hadn't she considered Wes's feelings?

"Wes, I didn't mean—"

"Yes, you did, Laurel. I saw you hesitate. But I get it. This is new territory for both of us. Yet while I may be leaving for a year, I *will* be back. So you'd better get used to it." He kissed Sarah-Jane's cheek. "I'll see you later, sweetheart."

Laurel's stomach twisted like a pretzel as she watched him walk away. How selfish could she be? The pastor and most everyone else in town knew she was a single mother and that she'd never been married. So why had she been so afraid to tell the truth about Wes? And how would that decision impact Sarah-Jane?

Her eyes momentarily closed. *Oh, Lord, please help me find a way to make this right.*

Wes eased his truck to a stop in front of Irma's house a few hours later, after lunch with Rae. He'd never been prouder than when Laurel referred to him as Sarah-Jane's daddy yesterday. The way it seemed to just tumble out sounded so natural. So when she introduced him to the pastor as Rae's brother, it had felt like a kick in the gut. And here he'd thought their relationship was improving, especially after she'd told him about her own father yesterday.

Getting out of his truck, he threw the door closed and started up the walk, eyeing a squirrel that darted across the lawn. He had done everything he could to assure her he was all in for Sarah-Jane. Yet Laurel still didn't trust him. Either that, or she didn't want him in the picture. Didn't want someone else to have a say in Sarah-Jane's life. Laurel was used to going it alone, after all. What if she saw him as a threat? One she hoped to stop.

He would not let that happen.

What can I do when I'm half a world away?

The only thing he could—trust God to go to battle for him.

With a sigh, he climbed the steps onto Irma's front porch. Yesterday things had appeared so promising. Now he and Laurel had to find a way around this new pothole in their relationship.

Unlocking the front door, he strode inside the old Victorian home, noting that the humidity in the house had lowered considerably. Just what he'd been hoping for when he decided to keep the place closed up for the weekend, leaving the blowers and air conditioner running for the past forty-eight hours. The lower the humidity, the faster things would dry out.

After depositing the keys and his notepad atop the nearest box in the parlor, he retrieved the moisture meter from his back pocket and headed into the family room, where the bulk of the water had been. Fortunately, the joists that remained had only been impacted by water from the collapse itself, as opposed to the wood that had been absorbing moisture from the leak for who knew how long. That wood now rested at the bottom of the dumpster in Irma's driveway.

The drywall was another concern, however. Despite having pulled off the baseboards that first day, it was hard to tell how much water could have leached up any given wall prior to that.

Dropping to one knee on the wooden floor, he touched the sensor pins to a lower section of the wall that had been home to the bookcases. Pleased with the reading, he tested one of the wooden planks on the floor. Damage to the floors had actually been one of his greatest fears. If any of them were warped, they'd have to be sanded and refinished. Not only would that take more time than he had, it also meant Irma would be displaced even longer. His hope was that, since they'd been able to attack things so quickly with the shop vacs, they'd be fine. And from the looks of things in the family room, it appeared he just may have gotten his wish.

He continued with the meter, into the hallway and around to the bedroom, until he was convinced they'd actually be able to get started on the repairs this week. Then he returned to the parlor and scooped up his notepad to start making a list of supplies.

"Hello."

Wes lifted his head at the unfamiliar voice.

"Wes, are you in here?"

Leaving his notes atop a box, he turned and moved into the entry hall to see Pastor Kleinschmidt poking his head through the door.

"Oh, there you are." The man who looked to be ten to fifteen years older than Wes's forty years smiled and slipped inside. "I knocked, but I guess you didn't hear it."

"No, these air movers make it kind of difficult to hear anything." They practically had to yell to be heard. "Stand by." With that, Wes moved into the bedroom and family room to turn off the units, all the while wondering why the pastor would be looking for him.

With only the hushed sounds of the blowers upstairs remaining, he rejoined the man in the entry hall.

"Your sister told me you were here." The pastor's suit from this morning had been replaced with jeans and a polo shirt, and a pair of sunglasses were perched atop his bald head, making him appear much more casual. "I hope you don't mind me just dropping by like this."

"Not at all." Though Wes was definitely curious.

The man's dark gaze drifted to the parlor, his eyes widening as he took in everything from furniture to boxes to a queen-size mattress. "Looks like you all had quite an undertaking."

"We certainly did, especially since time was of the essence. But thanks to your congregation, we got it done quicker than I'd ever imagined."

"They are a wonder. I'm just sorry I wasn't able to help out." He looked at Wes. "I was down in south Texas at a church conference."

"Well, it's not like anyone planned for this, but God provided. And, thankfully, Irma wasn't injured."

"That's for sure." The man shook his head. "I'm also grateful God placed you here in Bliss at just the right time. Your willingness to help a stranger says a lot about your character, Wes."

Too bad Laurel didn't see things that way.

He shrugged. "It'll give me something to do while I'm here."

"Oh, I'm sure you've got plenty to keep you busy. Spending time with your sister...and Sarah-Jane."

His gaze shot to the pastor's.

"Laurel sought me out after you left and filled me in on the rest of your story."

Despite the man's matter-of-fact tone, Wes shifted from one booted foot to the next. "She...she did that?" Suddenly he had that uneasy feeling that must've kept Laurel from telling the truth in the first place. Owning up to sin was always tough. Admitting to that sin in front of a man of God was downright unnerving. "I only learned about Sarah-Jane after coming to Bliss. Laurel and I, well, it shouldn't have happened."

The pastor held up his hands. "I'm not here to judge,

Wes. That's God's job. The good news is that He's a gracious God Who can turn even our biggest mistakes into our greatest blessings."

"He certainly did in this case. Sarah-Jane is..." Watching the rainbow of colors the sun's rays cast through the front door's leaded glass, he pondered how to describe how he felt about his daughter. "She's a blessing I'm not sure I deserve."

"God must not have seen it that way, Wes. Otherwise He wouldn't have brought you to Bliss."

"Humph. I thought the same thing myself. The part about Him bringing me to Bliss, anyway."

"Well, there are no coincidences where God is concerned. Which brings me to the real reason I came by." Hands perched casually on his hips, the pastor kept his focus on Wes. "We're having a men's prayer breakfast at the church on Saturday morning, and I wanted to extend an invitation. I was hoping that, perhaps, you could share what it is you'll be doing in the mission field. Give our men the opportunity to pray for you."

The notion of standing up and talking to a bunch of strangers made Wes a little uncomfortable. However, it wasn't like he was going on vacation. He was going to a war-torn country where peace was about as fragile as fine antique crystal. So, yeah, he'd take all the prayers he could get.

"I appreciate that. Yes, I can make it."

"Great. We meet in the fellowship hall at 7:00 a.m."

"I'll be there."

The pastor reached for the door. "Oh, and come hungry. We'll have a lot more than just doughnuts."

Wes chuckled. "Sounds good to me."

Watching the man retreat, Wes felt like a heel for

coming down so hard on Laurel. Yes, he was just being honest, and yes, he was hurt, but he could have been a little more tactful. At this rate, he would never earn her trust.

Chapter Nine

In south central Texas, a seventy-five-degree day without the threat of spring storms was one to savor. And Bliss had had its share of glorious days lately. Yet while this one had started out promising, things had quickly gone downhill for Laurel. Ever since that falling-out with Wes, she'd been in a funk. All because she'd been afraid to tell the pastor the truth. Even though she'd since corrected that faux pas, she was still out of sorts because she had no clue how to smooth things over with Wes.

After Sarah-Jane's nap, Laurel loaded her daughter into the stroller, and they were now on their way to Joyce's to inform Irma of the tentative timeline for the work on her house. Perhaps the visit would help improve Laurel's mood.

"She's getting so big." Irma watched Sarah-Jane walk into Joyce's 1970s ranch-style house, holding on to Laurel's hand.

"This walking thing is brand-new, too." Laurel directed her daughter toward the living room to their right, trying not to think about those first steps she'd taken to Wes. "Where's Joyce?"

"She had a family reunion in Austin today."

Laurel scanned the space, eyeing the dark paneled walls and mottled tan carpet as she searched for Joyce's dog. "I'm guessing she took Henry with her."

"Yes." Irma perched on the edge of the brown-and-gold sofa. "She treats that pup like it's her baby."

Still holding Sarah-Jane's hand, Laurel joined her friend. "I wanted to give you a heads-up on what's happening over at your place." She watched the way Irma's dark eyes lit as Sarah-Jane moved toward her. "Seems you had a little termite problem in that upstairs bathroom, so Frank Wurzbach will be by tomorrow to treat the wood. Once that's done, Wes can get started on the repairs. We're also going to do a little painting for you in the family room and bedroom to freshen those spaces."

"Oh—" Irma reached her hands out for Sarah-Jane to grab hold "—that would be lovely."

"Now about that carpet in the bedroom."

Irma gave Laurel her full attention then. "Good riddance is all I have to say about that."

Laurel couldn't help laughing at the demure woman's adamant tone. "We'll need to decide what we want to do in its stead. Do you want to replace the carpet or stick with just the wood floors and, perhaps, a large area rug?"

The conversation continued as Irma vacillated on whether area rugs were a good idea for someone her age.

"I still can't believe Wes is willing to do all of this work for me." The older woman lifted Sarah-Jane into her lap. "He's supposed to be visiting his sister, after all. But then, he is headed into the mission field. That right there tells me he has a giving heart."

"Yeah, Wes is a good guy."

Twisting, Irma lifted a brow. "Do I detect a hint of attraction, Laurel?"

Laurel felt her eyes widen. "What? No. I mean, maybe at one time, but—I don't date. My daughter is my focus." Unlike Laurel's mother, whose dates sometime lasted for weeks.

"What do you mean 'at one time'? Were you and Wes in a relationship before?"

Laurel bit her lip. She'd stepped in it now. "No, no relationship. Just..." Did she dare tell Irma? She'd already told the pastor. And as word got out—not that Laurel thought the pastor was going to go blabbing—Irma would hear about it anyway and be hurt that Laurel hadn't told her herself.

Sarah-Jane reached for Laurel then. Taking hold of her, Laurel said, "Irma, Wes is Sarah-Jane's father. It was a chance meeting in Las Vegas two years ago."

"Oh. Well. Evidently what they say isn't true then, because what happened in Vegas did not remain there."

Laurel puffed out a laugh as she smoothed a hand over her daughter's soft hair. "No, it definitely followed me home."

"Did Wes know about Sarah-Jane?"

Laurel grimaced. "Not until five days ago."

"I see. Well, that does complicate things, doesn't it?" The older woman didn't act the least bit put off by Laurel's news.

"Tell me about it. Not only did he turn out to be Rae's brother, but I didn't expect him to be so willing to embrace his role as a father."

"But that's a good thing for Sarah-Jane, don't you agree?" Her dark eyes were fixed on Laurel.

"I suppose." Biting her lip, Laurel couldn't help

thinking about all the ups and downs of these past few days as she and Wes tried to find a level playing ground.

"You don't want to share her, do you?"

"Would you want to share your baby with a stranger?"

"You must have seen something good in him at one time."

Laurel thought back to their first meeting, when she'd tried to pay him for that Coke. She'd been so embarrassed.

"I have to do something to say thank you."

"No, you don't." He briefly looked away, as though he was nervous. "However, I just ordered up a big basket of wings. I'd welcome the company, if you'd care to join me."

When he'd looked at Laurel again, there had been an honesty in his eyes she wasn't accustomed to seeing in people. Wes had never set out to impress her or anyone else. And that had endeared her to him more than she wanted to admit. Even to herself.

"He was kind," she finally said. "A good listener. He's the one who gave me the courage to leave my corporate job and follow my dream of starting my own company." A sigh escaped her lips. "He was unlike any guy I'd ever met."

Irma's brow hiked a little higher. "And you're not interested why?"

Laurel shook her head. "Doesn't matter, Irma." She stood, bringing her daughter with her. "Like I said, I don't date."

After bidding Irma goodbye, Laurel returned Sarah-Jane to her stroller and pushed her home, trying not to dwell on all those wonderful things she'd remembered about Wes. Yet when she arrived at her house, he was on her front porch.

"There you are." Turning, he started down the steps as anxiety rose inside Laurel.

"We, uh, went over to see Irma so I could update her on things." She peered up at him. "I didn't expect to see you today." Then again, he probably just wanted to spend time with Sarah-Jane.

"I owe you an apology for acting like a jerk at church."

"You weren't a jerk. You—" Lowering her gaze, she noticed something in his hands. "What's in the bag?"

"A peace offering." He held it up. "Butter pecan ice cream."

Her favorite. And if memory served her correctly— "Isn't that your favorite, too?"

"You remembered."

Unfortunately, after talking with Irma, she remembered far more than she wanted.

"You take this—" he handed her the bag "—and I'll free Sarah-Jane."

She looked inside the bag as he unhooked the clasps. "Blue Bell. You got the good stuff."

He lifted his daughter to him as though he'd done it all of Sarah-Jane's life. "That's the official ice cream of Texas, right?"

"If it's not, it should be." She started up the steps. "Come on in."

In the kitchen, she set the ice cream on the counter and grabbed two bowls from the cupboard. "Wes, I'm the one who owes you an apology. I should have told the pastor who you were to Sarah-Jane and me instead of trying to cover."

"It did sting." Still holding Sarah-Jane, he watched

her from the other side of the peninsula. "But I understand why you did it."

Reaching for an ice cream scoop, she watched, waiting for him to continue.

"I ran into the pastor at Irma's. He told me you sought him out after I left. Knowing the pastor knew what had happened between us was a little unnerving."

She scooped ice cream into the first bowl. "What did he say?"

"He said it wasn't his place to judge. And that he was there to invite me to speak at some men's prayer breakfast." He paused then, his forehead furrowing as though he was distressed. "Has anyone ever judged you for being a single mom?"

"I suppose there may have been a few eyebrows raised along the way. But by and large, the people of Bliss have been nothing but good to me."

"Good. I'd hate to think of someone treating you badly." The look on his face, the sincerity in his voice… That was why she'd fallen for this man. Except things had been safe in Vegas. She knew she'd be leaving the next morning, so she didn't have to worry about getting her heart broken when he turned his back on her. And if she didn't watch herself, she was apt to fall again. Only this time, she was certain not to come out unscathed.

Wes stood at the double front doors of Joyce's sprawling rambler Tuesday evening, wishing he'd had the nerve to turn down Irma's dinner invitation when she'd stopped by her house earlier in the day. But when she'd started talking about love languages and how hers was cooking and dinner was the only way she'd be able to properly thank him for all he was doing, well, he couldn't bring himself to say no.

So here he stood, holding a bouquet of flowers he'd picked up at the grocery store, feeling like he'd been summoned by the admiral.

He sucked in a breath, worked the kinks out of his neck and lifted his hand to knock.

She's a nice lady who just wants to say thank you.

That's right. Except Joyce would probably be here, too. That woman would give Rae a run for her money when it came to interrogation. Rae was less intimidating, though.

He swallowed hard and was about to knock when he heard a vehicle behind him. Turning, he saw Laurel's SUV rolling to a stop in the circular drive of the brick house. Had she been invited, too?

Man, he hoped so.

She emerged from the vehicle, eyeing him over its roof. "What are you doing here?"

"I was invited for dinner."

"Huh. Sarah-Jane and I were, too." Tossing her door closed, she opened the back door to retrieve their daughter.

Wes joined her. "Let me guess, Irma wanted to say thank you for helping her?"

Her gray-green eyes met his. "Cooking is her love language, you know?"

He couldn't help laughing. "So I've been told."

"Were you able to get those joists replaced?" Approaching the door, she cast him a sideways glance.

"Yep, they're all in." Yesterday the wood had been treated for termites, allowing Wes to get in there today with the replacements. "And the plumber will be by in the morning to work on the pipes. After that, things are in my hands."

The front door opened as they approached, and a little white dog wandered outside.

"I thought I heard voices out here." Joyce's gaze moved between them. "You two are right on time." She held the door wide, allowing them to enter.

Sarah-Jane twisted in Laurel's arms, seemingly fixated on the dog.

"Come on, Henry." Joyce waved the animal inside, too.

"These are for you." Wes held out the flowers. "Or Irma." He hesitated, feeling like a fool. "Who's doing the cooking?"

"We both pitched in." The corners of Joyce's mouth quirked upward.

"That's good—" still holding a distracted Sarah-Jane, Laurel leaned in "—because the flowers are for both of you to enjoy."

Phew. He'd have to remember to thank her later.

Laurel set Sarah-Jane on the floor and held her hand as they followed Joyce and some very enticing aromas into the outdated kitchen. Obviously the '70s weren't lost on Joyce. Orange, brown and gold dominated every surface, including the countertops.

"Hello, hello." Standing beside the ancient downdraft cooktop, Irma waved before shifting her attention to her friend. "Joyce, which serving bowl would you like me to use for these mashed potatoes?"

"It's right up—" Still holding the flowers, Joyce turned toward him. "Wes, would you mind getting that bowl for me?" She opened the dark walnut cupboard over the pass-through to the family room and pointed to the top shelf.

"Sure." He reached to grab it.

"It's so nice to have a man around," he heard Irma say behind him. "Wouldn't you agree, Laurel?"

Handing the bowl to Irma, he couldn't help noticing the pink that had crept into Laurel's cheeks.

A short time later, they moved into the dark wood-paneled dining room for a meal of chicken fried steak, mashed potatoes, corn and broccoli. Laurel settled Sarah-Jane into the waiting high chair before taking the seat beside it, while Wes pulled out a high-backed chair across from her.

"Why, thank you, Wes." Joyce eased into the seat, leaving him standing there, feeling like a bump on a log. As Irma took the chair beside her, Joyce looked up at him. "You can sit next to Laurel."

He wasn't about to argue. Not that he minded sitting beside Laurel, but this was turning into one really awkward evening. Especially when Irma insisted they all hold hands while they said grace.

"Wes, what are your plans when you come back from Iraq?" Irma cut into her meat.

With a bite of mashed potatoes waiting on his fork, he said, "Well, I have a year to consider my options, so I'm not a hundred percent certain yet."

"You'll be coming back to Bliss, though. Right?" There was a sense of urgency in Irma's voice. "I mean, Sarah-Jane needs her father."

Laurel nearly choked on the sip of water she'd been in the midst of swallowing.

Lowering his fork, he passed her a napkin, this whole evening suddenly becoming crystal clear. Laurel must have confided in Irma. Now the woman—his gaze drifted to an expectant Joyce—make that *women* were doing everything they could to bring him and Laurel together.

"Yes, ma'am. I am definitely considering making a home in Bliss."

Joyce set down her fork. "Laurel, have I shown you my granddaughter's wedding photos?"

Boy, talk about subtle.

"No, but—"

The white-haired woman stood and retrieved something from the adjoining living room. "It was such a lovely spring wedding."

"Spring weddings are always nice." Irma watched as Joyce handed a stack of pictures to Laurel. "But then, fall weddings are beautiful, too." She chuckled. "Come to think of it, there's really not a bad time for a wedding. Except maybe Christmas. Everyone is so busy then." She regarded Laurel. "Laurel, when do you think is the perfect time to get married?"

Flipping through the photos, her eyes went wide. "Um, I guess I've never thought about it."

"Of course you have," Joyce corrected. "Every young girl dreams of her wedding."

"Sorry." Laurel handed the pictures back. "I'm too busy being a mom to think about a wedding." She offered Sarah-Jane a bite of mashed potatoes, but the child only had eyes for the dog pacing around her chair. "I think somebody is quite smitten with Henry."

"Can't say as I blame her." Joyce scooted her chair away from the table. "I am, too." Rounding the table, she looked down at the dog. "If you'll be nice to Sarah-Jane, I'll take you outside so the two of you can play."

"I'll help." Irma was on her feet in no time.

"That's all right." Laurel pushed her chair away from the table. "I can go with her."

"Nonsense." Irma patted her on the shoulder. "You and Wes stay here and enjoy your dinner. *Alone.*"

Laurel looked as though she wanted to crawl under a rock. As the women departed with Sarah-Jane, she dropped her head in her hands. "This is my fault."

"Why do you say that?"

"I told Irma you're Sarah-Jane's father." Lifting her head, she pushed the hair out of her face.

"You told the pastor, too."

"Yes, but he's not prone to playing matchmaker."

"Oh. Well, at least they're great cooks." He ate another bite of steak.

Laurel scanned the table. "I guess we could clear the dishes."

"And ruin our *alone* time?"

Her laugh was genuine. She sure was pretty when she did that. "You know, if you do move to Bliss, you can expect more of this."

"Dinners?"

"Matchmaking." She stabbed a piece of broccoli with her fork. "These ladies, not to mention several others, have been beside themselves since Rae, Paisley, Christa and I came to town." She took a bite.

"Fresh meat?"

"Pretty much. At least I have Sarah-Jane to use as an excuse."

"You mean, no dates?"

Setting her fork on her plate, she grabbed her glass and leaned back. "I've never been much into the whole dating scene."

"Why not?"

She shrugged. "After my dad left, my mom spent her life bouncing from guy to guy, thinking one of them would make her happy. I'd rather make my own happiness."

"My parents had a great marriage." He wasn't sure

why he said that, but he kept going anyway. "They always seemed so in sync with each other. That didn't mean they didn't each have their own goals and desires, but they supported each other and had similar values that permeated everything they did."

"You were blessed to have such a great example."

"Yeah." He foolishly allowed his mind to drift back to before the accident. "I used to hope I'd find a partner like that one day." He probably shouldn't have said that out loud.

"Does that mean you stopped?"

"I guess my dream died when they did." At least, until he met Laurel.

"Sarah-Jane—" Joyce chuckled somewhere in the vicinity of the kitchen "—we'll just have to talk to your mama about getting you a puppy."

And just like that, the moment was gone. But not before Wes realized that Laurel could be the partner he'd always dreamed of.

Chapter Ten

After dropping Sarah-Jane with her regular sitter Mary Lou on Wednesday morning, Laurel headed over to Bliss Hardware with thoughts of last night still tumbling through her mind.

Why didn't she date? Because she was afraid of falling in love and having her heart broken. Between her mother and her father, she'd endured enough rejection. There was no way she'd tell Wes that, though. No matter how much she might want to. Instead, she needed to work harder at keeping her heart in check. Especially after Wes had all but said he'd given up on the idea of marriage.

I guess my dream died when they did.

Dreams were fragile things. One little slip and they could shatter into a million pieces.

"All right, your color gurus are present and accounted for." Paisley's sweet southern drawl was unmistakable.

Laurel tore her gaze away from the wall of paint chips to hug Christa and Paisley. Since Christa owned Bliss Hardware and Paisley had a flair for decorating that would put even professional designers to shame, it seemed only logical that they help her choose the paint colors for Irma's bedroom, bath and family room.

"You must be busy at Irma's." Christa slid her hands into the back pockets of her jeans. "I've barely seen you since that day Mildred ran you down."

At the moment, that whole incident seemed like forever ago. Yet it had only been nine days. And, my, how things had changed since then.

"I couldn't help noticing you sitting beside Rae's brother at church on Sunday." Paisley lifted two perfectly arched brows. "Wesley sure is easy on the eyes."

A grinning Christa added, "I heard he's doing the repairs at Irma's, too, so I guess the two of you are spending a *lot* of time together."

Before Laurel could cringe at the implications, she realized that she'd not told them about Wes. What kind of friend was she, telling a matchmaking Irma when she hadn't even told her best friends?

"Oh boy." She rubbed her forehead.

"What is it, darlin'?" Paisley took a step closer.

Shifting her attention to Christa, Laurel said, "Any chance we could talk in your office?"

"Sure." Christa's hazel gaze narrowed. "Is everything all right?"

"Yes, there's just something I need to tell the both of you."

Christa wasted no time in hustling them across the store, past the power tools, hummingbird feeders and door locks.

"Annie," she hollered over her shoulder to the gal behind the counter, "I'll be in my office for a bit."

While the rest of Bliss Hardware was very utilitarian, Christa's office had a cozy farmhouse vibe going on, with warm white shiplap walls, a colorful area rug and a modern-yet-rustic wooden desk with a sawhorse-style base.

Laurel eased into one of two trendy metal side chairs as Christa closed the door in such a hurry that the black-and-white-checkered valance over its window stuck straight out for a moment.

Paisley took the second chair, crossing her denim-covered legs, her cornflower blue eyes fixed on Laurel. "All right, darlin', what's going on?"

With Christa leaning her backside against the desk, Laurel looked from one friend to the other. "Wes is Sarah-Jane's father." Saying it seemed to be getting easier, though the looks on her friends' faces had her wincing.

"How long have you known this?"

Paisley shot Christa an annoyed look. "I can't believe you asked that."

Christa cringed. "I know. That didn't come out right."

"I'll say." Paisley shifted her attention back to Laurel. "The question is, how long has Wesley known?"

"Oh, a little over a week now."

"You know—" Christa's mouth twisted "—that day at the café, I thought there was something familiar about him."

Laurel and Paisley both looked at her.

"His eyes! Sarah-Jane has his eyes."

"That she does," Laurel conceded.

"I'm assuming Rae knows." Paisley's gaze seemed riveted to Laurel's.

"Yes. Our perceptive friend managed to pretty much figure it out on her own."

"Wow." Christa pushed away from the desk and began to pace. "This is just crazy."

"You're telling me." Standing, Laurel crossed to the

row of two-drawer white file cabinets against the opposite wall and grabbed a piece of chocolate from the small galvanized bucket labeled In Case of Emergency.

"What are the two of you going to do?" Paisley cocked her head, sending her red hair spilling over one shoulder. "Now that Wes knows, is he going to pay child support? Do you think he'll want partial custody?" She held up a finger. "Wait, he's on his way overseas."

Laurel tore the golden wrapper away from the candy. "I think each of those topics has been touched on at some point. But, for now, he and Sarah-Jane are just getting acquainted." She bit into the chocolate, caramel and cookie goodness.

"And how is that going?" Ankles crossed, Paisley gripped the sides of her chair.

When she'd finished chewing, Laurel said, "Quite well, actually. Sarah-Jane took to him right away. Oh, and she's finally walking. Her first steps were in an effort to get to him."

Christa fingered through the bucket now, in search of her favorite candy. "And how do you feel about that?"

"I'm…conflicted." Laurel returned to her chair. "On the one hand, I want Sarah-Jane to know her father. To have a relationship with him." One shoulder lifted. "I mean, I've dreamed of that for myself my entire life. But at the same time, I'm afraid for her. What if Wes decides he doesn't want to be a father? What if he goes away and never comes back?"

"The way your father did." Paisley watched her.

Lips pursed, Laurel simply nodded.

"Well, cautious is good." Christa tossed her candy wrapper in the trash. "After all, we don't call you Mama Bear for nothing."

Paisley remained silent, looking rather thoughtful.

"You're too quiet, Paise." Christa dropped into her desk chair. "What's going on in that pretty head of yours?"

"I don't want the two of you jumping all over me for this, however, I am the romantic in our little group."

"Here we go again." Christa rolled her eyes and spun her chair around.

"Laurel?" Paisley's gaze bore into her. "Is there any chance you, Wes and Sarah-Jane could be a real family? Not right now, but eventually."

Christa brought her chair to an abrupt stop. "You think Laurel and Wes should get married?" While Paisley may be the romantic one, matters of the heart never seemed to blip on Christa's radar. At forty-two, Christa not only had never been married, but she was adamant that she never would. Probably why she and Laurel got on so well.

"Not right now," Paisley was quick to add. "But somewhere down the road, maybe after he gets back from Iraq?"

Laurel reached for her friend's hand. "Paisley, I love that you're a romantic, and I wish I were more like you, but no. I'm not interested in settling down with Wes or anyone else. And neither is Wes."

Both pairs of eyes settled on her.

Christa's were round. "Does that mean you've discussed it?"

Maybe in a roundabout way, last night at Joyce's, but Laurel wasn't going to bring that up. "No. But Rae says Wes thinks he doesn't deserve a family."

"Because he believes he's responsible for their parents' deaths." Paisley nodded. "I've heard her say that, too. So sad."

"Except he does have a family." Christa shrugged.

"Two, actually. First it was he and Rae, and now he has Sarah-Jane."

"This is true," said Paisley. "So, as he spends more time with Sarah-Jane and, by extension, you, he could change his mind." She looked at Laurel. "What would you do then?"

Either fall into his arms or run the other way.

"Look, we could sit here and play what-ifs all day long." She pushed out of her chair. "But we have work to do." Jerking the door opened, she added, "So are y'all going to help me pick out paint colors or what?"

By three o'clock that afternoon, the plumber had finally finished repiping the upstairs bathroom. Unfortunately, he hadn't been able to get there as early as Wes would have liked, thanks to an emergency at one of the businesses in town, which left Wes to putz around with whatever he could find, trying not to think about Laurel. Yet no matter what he did, he couldn't get her out of his mind.

If last night had shown him anything, it was that he and Laurel were cut from the same cloth. Both were determined to avoid romantic relationships. Yet here they were with a daughter. How was it they'd both wavered from their resolve that night in Vegas? And why couldn't he seem to stop thinking about her?

He needed to work, to occupy his mind with something besides the pretty blonde accountant and the adorable baby they shared, because the two of them together created too tempting a picture. One he wasn't worthy of. His parents had paid for his mistakes with their lives. Rae had sacrificed because of those same mistakes and he wasn't willing to put anyone else he cared about in jeopardy.

Standing in Irma's upstairs bathroom, he studied the hole that was now crisscrossed with wood and PVC pipe. Tomorrow he'd add the subfloor up here and drywall to the ceiling below. He wasn't sure what Laurel had planned for flooring in the bathroom, but once the subfloor was in, he could safely remove the old sheet vinyl without fear of ending up in the family room.

"Wes?" Laurel's voice drifted from the entry hall downstairs.

As if he hadn't spent enough time with her already today. She just wasn't aware of it.

"Up here."

A few moments later, she stood in the doorway, wearing a pair of skinny jeans, a maroon Texas A&M T-shirt and a pair of slip-on canvas sneakers. With her blond waves spilling over her shoulders, she was about the prettiest worker he'd ever seen.

"How's it going?"

"Well, the plumber finished." He pointed toward the hole in the floor.

She tiptoed into the small space.

"Careful—"

Before he could finish his warning, her foot caught on a strip of the old flooring, and she lost her balance.

Wes made a quick side step and managed to catch her. "Sorry, I should have warned you sooner."

Her cheeks were red as she straightened. "I'm too clumsy for my own good."

With one arm still around her waist, he brushed the hair out of her face. "Clumsy never looked so beautiful." Or smelled so good.

Realizing what he'd just said, he let her go. Those were the things that had gotten them into trouble the first time around.

Regaining her composure, she shifted her gaze from the floor to him. "So, what's next?"

He explained his plans for tomorrow. "That reminds me, I haven't heard you mention what you're doing for flooring in here."

Her eyes went wide. "That's because it completely slipped my mind."

"Which means you probably don't have anyone lined up to install it, either."

"Of course I don't." Hands on her hips, she moved into the hall and began to pace. "And whatever I do decide on is probably going to take at least a week to get here." She groaned, planting a palm against her forehead. "I can't believe I forgot."

He hated to see her being so hard on herself. Joining her in the hallway, he said, "All right, let's just settle down for a second. First question, what do you envision on the floor in this bathroom? Sheet vinyl or something else? I mean, for an application like this, you could do vinyl plank or tile."

Stopping, she turned to face him. "Actually, I did have an idea."

He lifted a brow, waiting for her continue.

"I saw this woman on TV who renovates a lot of old houses and she always used those black-and-white mosaic tiles. You know, like the small squares or hexagons."

He nodded. "Yeah, I know what you're talking about. And you're right, that would look good in here. It's a small space, and the style would fit in with the character of the house."

"Much better than that faux-brick vinyl." She motioned toward the bath. "But where does one find something like that?"

"The big home improvement centers usually carry them."

"Really? That sounds easy enough."

"Yeah." He checked his watch. "And since there's really not much I can do here today, we could grab Sarah-Jane and make a run right now. Where is she, anyway?"

"At her regular sitter's. But why do we all need to go?"

"Well, *you* need to be there to make sure you get what you want, and if Sarah-Jane doesn't go, I won't get any time with her, since we'll likely be gone for a few hours. And finally, I'm the guy with the truck."

"Oh." The way her brow furrowed was dealing a blow to his ego.

"Plus, if we get the stuff now, I'll have time to install it myself."

Her suddenly hopeful gaze jerked to his. "You can do that?"

Now she was impressed. "When it comes to construction, there's not much I can't do, Laurel. Except those things that require a license, like plumbing and electrical. So, what do you say?"

"Let me pick up Sarah-Jane and I'll meet you at the house in thirty minutes."

Two and a half hours later, after a fast-food dinner they hoped would keep Sarah-Jane in a good mood, Wes pushed an industrial cart filled with backer board, mortar, tile, grout and everything else he would need to complete the flooring project in Irma's upstairs bath toward the checkout counter of the home improvement center. Of course, Laurel had to pause at least half a dozen times to look at home decor stuff. Wes didn't complain, though. He was having too much fun entertaining Sarah-Jane, who was strapped into the seat of a regular shopping cart. She really was a good baby. Always quick with a smile. And the fact that he seemed to be able to do no wrong in her eyes was an added bonus.

Darkness had already descended over Bliss by the time they made it back to Laurel's, and Sarah-Jane was asleep in her car seat.

"I'll get her," he told Laurel as she hopped out of the truck. Opening the back door, he carefully removed the straps that kept his daughter safe and lifted her to him.

With a contented sigh, she snuggled against him, and he couldn't help holding her a little tighter as they made their way toward the house.

Laurel ascended the porch before him and unlocked the front door.

Despite Laurel removing her little shoes and pants, Sarah-Jane remained asleep, even when he laid her in her crib.

"She must be tuckered out," he whispered to Laurel.

"All that excitement. You're quite the entertainer, you know." Laurel started for the door, but Wes couldn't seem to make himself move. Instead, he just stood there, watching his daughter sleep. So innocent. Such a precious gift from God.

He didn't know how long he'd been there when he felt a hand on his arm.

Laurel was beside him again. "I have done this same thing many a time. There's just something about a sleeping baby that's so peaceful."

His gaze lowered to his daughter. "Definitely."

When he managed to pull himself away, they moved into the hall, and Laurel softly closed the door behind them.

"I'm curious," he said as they moved into the living

room. "How did you come up with the name Sarah-Jane?"

"Sarah was my grandmother's name. It means princess." She gathered a few toys that littered the floor. "However, I like the name Jane because it means God is gracious." She tossed the toys into a basket before leaning against the end of the sofa. "I felt as though God had been so gracious, allowing me to be a mother to this little princess…" Though her voice cracked, she smiled, blinking repeatedly. "It just fit."

"Yes, it does." He longed to touch her, to let her know she wasn't in this alone. Instead, he shoved his hands into the pockets of his jeans. "Has Rae ever told you that Jane was our mother's name?"

Laurel straightened, her composure returning. "Now that you mention it, yes. I'd forgotten. Probably because it didn't mean as much then, but now…" She paused before looking up at him, blinking. "Wes, God's hand has been all over this baby's life, even when we were unaware."

"Yeah. And He brought me here, to Bliss." He studied the curve of her face, the freckles that dotted her nose. "You know, I've never forgotten you, Laurel. At the most random times, something you said or did would play across my mind."

"Like when I ordered you to bring me a Coke?"

He couldn't help laughing. "Oh, I've thought about that one a lot. But you didn't order me—you were very polite."

"I still can't believe you actually bought the drink yourself and brought it to me."

"Seeing you sitting there with your feet dangling in the pool in your tailored dress told me that you were not some high-powered exec who was used to getting her own way."

Standing, she tilted her head, watching him with such an intensity it nearly took his breath away. "What did it tell you?"

"That you appreciated the simple things in life. That you didn't take things too seriously and you liked to have fun."

"Wow, you're good."

He lifted a shoulder. "It's a gift."

"I thought construction was your gift."

"Can't a guy have more than one gift?"

"I think you have plenty, Wes Bishop. Including being a wonderful father."

"What makes you say that?"

"Because you're a man who genuinely cares and views being a part of his daughter's life as a privilege, not an obligation."

"It is definitely a privilege." Staring into her gray-green eyes, his throat clogged with emotion. Just knowing that was how she saw him meant more to him than she would ever know. And the feelings he had for her, the ones he'd been trying to squelch ever since that first day he saw her in the street, rose to the surface, refusing to be contained any longer.

He forced himself to look away. He wasn't worthy of Laurel's praise, any more than he was worthy of that precious little girl sleeping down the hall. Yet that hadn't stopped him from falling in love with his daughter. Now he was dangerously close to falling for her mother, too.

He couldn't let that happen.

Taking a step back, he said, "I need to run that stuff over to Irma's before it gets too late."

Chapter Eleven

Laurel set Sarah-Jane in her playard late the next afternoon, then headed into the kitchen to fill her sippy cup. Wes would be here soon, and that concerned Laurel even more than the ominous gray clouds gathering to the west. While she wasn't able to make it over to Irma's today because of work commitments, that hadn't kept her thoughts from drifting to Wes and their conversation last night.

She'd meant what she said about him being a wonderful father. She just wished she had kept that particular thought to herself, because the look in his eyes had nearly been her undoing. Coupled with that little stumble she'd taken at Irma's…

Filling Sarah-Jane's cup with water from the dispenser on the refrigerator, Laurel recalled the feel of Wes's strong arms around her and the way he made her feel safe, protected. The same way he had that night two years ago. No one else had ever made her feel like that before.

A knock at the front door startled her. She quickly put the lid on the cup and passed it to her daughter on her way through the living room where Wes, no doubt, stood on the other side of the door. Pausing, she drew in a deep breath. *Lord, help me to keep these crazy, mixed-up emotions in check.*

When she opened the door, though, the man on her porch wasn't Wes. He was older, tall, thin and clean-shaven with short gray hair. Hands in the pockets of his sharply creased medium-wash jeans, he looked nervous. And, while she couldn't put her finger on it, there was something familiar about him.

With Sarah-Jane safe in her playard, Laurel stepped into the humid air, pulling the door closed behind her. "Can I help you?"

He simply stared at her for a moment before saying, "Are you Laurel Donovan?"

"Yes."

The man's faded green eyes teared as a smile quivered at his lips. "My name is Jimmy Donovan."

Laurel felt her own eyes grow wide. Her nostrils flared as a jumbled ball of emotions slammed into her gut. Her breathing intensified. "*Get* out of here." Every muscle in her body tensed. How dare this…this—

"Please, let me—"

"No!" The word spewed from her mouth with a vehemence she'd never experienced. "I don't believe you." She dared a step closer, fists clenched. "What are you? Some kind of sicko? Have you been stalking me, gathering information so you can blackmail me or something?"

"No, I would never…" Lines creased his tanned brow, and he appeared confused. Panicked even. Yet he made no effort to move.

Fortunately for her, she spotted Wes's truck easing toward the curb. He'd take care of this pathetic excuse for a human being.

"You wait right there." Taking two steps back, she pointed toward the stranger, as though her finger alone would prevent him from fleeing.

To his credit, the guy looked genuinely freaked out as she motioned with her other hand for Wes to hurry.

Thankfully, Wes caught her drift, slammed his truck into Park and practically ran toward her, taking the porch steps in a single leap. "Is there a problem?"

"This—" she wagged her finger at the stranger "—this...*jerk* says he's my father."

Looking as though he'd pummel the guy if he made one wrong move, Wes cast a wary glare at the man. "State your business, sir." Suddenly Laurel was thankful Wes was a military man.

The stranger lifted his hands in the air. "My name is Jimmy—James—Donovan. I'm not here to make any trouble. I hired a private investigator to find my daughter, Laurel. You can check my ID and the returned letters I sent to her mother."

Laurel's heart squeezed, and she sucked in a sharp breath. "You have letters?"

"Yes." He kept one hand in the air while the other slowly reached for his back pocket.

Laurel shot a glance at Wes, who closely watched the man's every move like a lion ready to pounce.

The stranger's hand was shaking as he held out a small stack of envelopes.

Wes snatched them, giving them a quick once-over before passing them to Laurel.

Looking at the top one, she saw her mother's name, along with her grandmother's address and the words *Return to Sender.* Whether it was from the implications of these letters or the thunder rumbling in the distance, a shiver skittered down her spine.

With both hands again in the air, the stranger said, "My wallet with my ID is in my other pocket."

Wes didn't hesitate to retrieve it.

Confusion swirled through Laurel like gathering storm clouds as Sarah-Jane squawked inside. Could these letters be real? And what would it mean if they were?

She looked at Wes. "You okay for a minute?"

He nodded, pulling the man's ID from his wallet.

With a parting glance, she escaped inside, knowing she was not about to expose Sarah-Jane to this man Wes had in check. At least, she hoped he did. But considering how fit Wes was, her concern was probably for naught.

Moving around the sofa, she saw Sarah-Jane standing at the edge of her playard, holding on to her cup.

"What is it, baby?" Laurel set the envelopes on the counter and grabbed the small bowl of fish crackers. "Are you hungry?"

Her wide-eyed daughter did the "more" motion.

Even in the midst of this momentary crisis, Laurel couldn't help but smile. "I love you so much, baby." She kissed her daughter's head then handed her the bowl.

As Sarah-Jane plopped back down, curiosity pinged through Laurel's brain. What if this man was her father?

Retrieving the letters, she riffled through the small stack. Every one of them was postmarked thirty-two years ago. She would have been Sarah-Jane's age.

Setting the others aside, she opened the first envelope, pulled out a sheet of yellow legal paper and read.

"My beloved, Brenda. I miss you more than you will ever know, and I can't wait for you and Laurel to join me. I know I messed up but, thanks to your mother, I'm back on my feet. I'm working in the oil fields and am making more money than I ever imagined."

Something stopped her then. She again looked at the envelope.

Return to Sender. The writing was her grandmother's. She picked up the other four letters. They were all unopened with *Return to Sender* in her grandmother's script.

A sick feeling churned in Laurel's belly. Had her mother even seen these letters? And if what this man said was true, if he really was her father, where did she go from here?

Her eyes momentarily closed. *Lord, give me wisdom.*

With Sarah-Jane content, Laurel again slipped onto the porch. Wes was still on high alert, towering over the man who now sat on her wicker love seat, his hands in his lap, concern carving deep lines into his brow. And for the first time, she noticed that he looked…frail.

She drew in a bolstering breath, looking at Wes. "It's all right."

He nodded. "Are you okay if I check on Sa—?" His gaze momentarily shifted toward the stranger. "Our daughter?"

She appreciated his concern for Sarah-Jane. Not only that, but the way he said *our daughter* suggested that Laurel didn't live here alone. "Yes, I'll be fine."

With a parting glance, he said, "I'm right inside if you need me."

A multitude of questions played across her mind as she pulled up a chair and sat down opposite the man. She studied him a moment, realizing why he looked so familiar. It was his eyes, though she wasn't ready to admit how much they looked like hers.

"If you are my father, why didn't you try to find me sooner or come back to see me when I was little?

I mean, couldn't you have at least called? Didn't you want to see me?"

"More than you can imagine. And yes, I did think about coming back, wanting to reclaim what was rightfully mine." He shook his head repeatedly. "But shortly after those letters were returned to me, I received another envelope with divorce papers. Your mother had signed them and expected me to do the same." Something akin to heartache passed across his expression. "It about killed me, but I figured she'd moved on, so I signed them and sent 'em off."

Try as she might, Laurel was struggling to understand what he was saying. It was as though she was trying to put together a puzzle with only half of the pieces. "That doesn't make any sense. You left me and Mom without even saying goodbye."

His shoulders slumped. "Is that what they told you?"

She nodded. "Mom said you went to jail, and when you got out, she never heard from you again."

He dragged a weathered hand over his face. "I guess I'd better start from the beginning. That is, if you have time." He nodded toward the door. "With the little one and all."

"She's with her father." Laurel had never imagined herself saying that before. Or that she'd be sitting on her porch with a man that could possibly be *her* father. "And yes, I need to know the whole story." Not that she was ready to believe everything this stranger said.

Drawing in a deep breath, he stared out across the lawn as clouds overtook what had been a brilliant blue sky. "Your mother and me, we were young. Fell in love in high school and married before the ink was dry on our diplomas. Of course, your grandmother wasn't real pleased about the fact that we snuck off to the justice of the peace as opposed to having a formal church wedding. But we didn't care. We had big dreams for ourselves."

Laurel leaned back in her chair, though she was anything but relaxed as she tried to envision a younger version of this man and her mother together. "Such as?"

"I wanted to work in the oil industry. Wanted to build my own company. But then your mother got pregnant and couldn't work for a while when the doctor put her on bed rest. I managed to pull some overtime with my warehouse job, but the company folded shortly after you were born, and your mother got let go from her job." He met her gaze now. "My pride took a major hit when we had to move in with your grandmother. Don't get me wrong, I was grateful to Sarah Corwin for giving us a roof over our heads, but I wanted to provide for my family, and those temporary jobs I'd been taking weren't cutting it." His expression clouded. "I got desperate and started selling drugs, thinking I could make some fast money. Ended up going to jail instead. I spent the next six months trying to come up with a way to take care of my family, but when you're on the inside, the future doesn't always look so bright. Then, shortly before I was released, your grandmother came to see me and made me an offer."

Laurel's gaze narrowed. "What kind of offer?"

"She said Brenda had told her about my desire to work in the oil fields and that she'd talked to a man who was willing to hire me as a roughneck. Said she'd cover my fine and pay for a bus ticket and two weeks' worth of hotel, but I'd have to leave the moment I was released or else the fella would give the job to someone else."

Laurel recalled her grandmother's handwriting on

those envelopes. "You mean, you couldn't even say goodbye to us?"

"Your grandmother said there wasn't time, that I had to be on that first bus out. So I thanked her and promised I wouldn't let her down." The way his voice trailed off made it seem as though that was the end of the story.

Laurel gripped the arms of her chair. "Okay, so what happened then?"

"Everything came together just the way your grandmother had said. I got out, moved to west Texas and became a roughneck."

"All right, but what about my mom and me?"

Elbow on the arm of the settee, he rubbed a finger across his lips as tears again filled his eyes. "I never saw either one of you again." His voice cracked, making his sorrow seem so deep and real.

Despite the increasing thunder that seemed to insist she go inside, Laurel wasn't ready. There were things she still needed to know. "Did my mother visit you while you were in jail?"

He lifted a shoulder. "Not very often. But then, she had you to care for. After your grandmother's visit, I wrote Brenda a letter, explaining the plan, and told her I'd bring the two of you out to be with me just as soon as I had a place for us to live."

Laurel was almost afraid to ask. "So why didn't you send for us?"

"I did." He gave a slight shake of his head. "But the letter was returned just like the others."

Laurel's head was swimming. She'd thought that hearing the whole story would help clarify things, but her mind kept going back to her grandmother's handwriting on those envelopes. If what this man—Jimmy—said was true, then her grandmother had sabotaged her parents' marriage. And everything Laurel had ever believed was a lie.

The wind kicked up then, tinged with the smell of ozone.

She needed to go inside before the storm hit. But not before she had the answer to one last question. "Why did you decide to find me now?"

He stood, as though he was ready to evade the storm, too. "Because I'm dying."

Chapter Twelve

Wes was up early Friday morning. Not that he'd gotten much sleep. He was worried about Laurel. Having her father show up after thirty-plus years had to be a huge shock—even more so than when Wes first appeared in Bliss.

After the man left, Wes had remained at Laurel's until the thunderstorm had passed. At least that had been his excuse. Truth was, he wanted to be there in case Laurel needed him. Instead, he'd spent his time entertaining Sarah-Jane and making sure both she and Laurel ate.

What Laurel wanted, though, was to be alone. She'd been in a daze, no doubt processing the information she'd been given. Wes had no clue what was in those letters Jimmy Donovan gave Laurel, but there must have been some facts that were difficult to ignore, otherwise she wouldn't have spent so much time talking with him.

Wes was just glad he was there to take care of Sarah-Jane because, as of right now, Wes didn't want that man anywhere near his daughter. After returning to Rae's, Wes had spent the rest of the evening researching the person who claimed to be Laurel's father. He even sent the photo he'd taken of Jimmy's driver's license to an old navy buddy who worked for the FBI, but Wes had yet to hear anything.

Now, armed with two large Americanos, he headed to Laurel's a little before eight. After he'd told Rae what had transpired last night, his sister had encouraged him to give Laurel time, saying she'd talk when she was ready. But he wanted to see for himself how she was doing. If nothing else, it would at least alleviate his anxiety.

When he pulled up to the bluish-gray Craftsman-style home, he put his truck in Park and paused. *Dear Lord, I know Laurel is confused and hurting right now. I pray that You will comfort her and give her wisdom to know the truth about this man who claims to be her father.*

Killing the engine, he grabbed the coffees and made his way up the walk. The morning sun filtered through the established trees. A few leaves littered the ground, the only evidence of last night's storm. The one out here, anyway.

At the door, he knocked, and Laurel opened it a few moments later with Sarah-Jane on her hip. Wearing black yoga pants and a two-sizes-too-large T-shirt, Laurel stared at him through puffy eyes. And her hair was a mess.

"I wasn't expecting you," she said.

"I know. But I thought you could use this." He held out a cup. "One Americano, just the way you like it." For a second, he thought she was going to turn him away. Then Sarah-Jane reached for him. "How about we trade?"

She hesitated a split second before taking her drink, leaving him a free arm to grab Sarah-Jane.

Following Laurel into the dining area, he dared to ask, "How are you doing?"

"Fine. I'm just busy." She set the cup on the counter and moved around the peninsula into the kitchen. "Sarah-Jane needs to eat so I can take her to the sitter."

"Oh. I thought she only went once a week?"

Laurel plucked a banana from the bunch on the counter. "I called Mary Lou this morning to see if she could take her again."

"Why?"

"Because I happen to have a job." She hastily opened the cabinet, grabbed a small plate, then let the door slam closed. "As if it's any of your business."

Oh, she was stressed, all right.

His phone dinged then, so while Laurel prepared Sarah-Jane's breakfast, he took his daughter into the living room to check the text he hoped was from his friend. Pulling the device from his pocket, he looked at the screen.

Check your email.

Just what Wes had been waiting for.

Opening the screen, he tapped a few buttons to bring up his email, then quickly scanned the information.

"Wes, I need Sarah-Jane in her high chair so she can eat."

"I'm on it." Turning, he closed the screen and tucked the phone away. "Are you hungry, sweetheart?"

She rubbed her chest.

"Mommy's gonna get you all fixed up." He slid the child into her seat.

"Wes, I appreciate the coffee, but I think you should go now." She set the plate with cut-up banana on Sarah-

Jane's tray then moved back into the kitchen, pausing at the refrigerator to grab the milk.

"Okay, but I'm a little confused as to why you're in such a hurry. Do you have a video chat or something?" Or did she simply want to wallow in the turmoil that was, no doubt, raging inside her? Since things had gotten better between them, he'd thought she might talk to him. Obviously he was mistaken.

"No." She removed the lid from a sippy cup. "I just need you to leave, all right?" She began to pour the milk with a shaky hand.

"Here—" he reached for the milk "—let me help you."

She jerked away, though, sending milk spilling onto the floor. Within seconds, her eyes filled with tears. She slammed the jug on the counter and grabbed a rag. "See what you made me do."

Wes quickly moved around the peninsula and tried to take the rag. "I can get this."

"No!" She jerked away again, but this time tears poured onto her cheeks. "I don't need your help." Her whole body shook. "I don't need anybody."

Wes couldn't take it anymore. Stepping over the small puddle, he wrapped his arms around Laurel.

Her body was rigid at first, but he refused to let go.

"Whether you need me or not, I'm here, Laurel. I'm here." Stroking her hair, he continued to hold her.

Finally, the tension seemed to flow from her, and she clung to him.

"I don't know what to believe." Her words were muffled against his shirt. "I'm so confused."

"Confused about what?" He didn't know if she'd confide in him or not, but he had to try.

A whimper sounded from Sarah-Jane.

"I must have scared her." Sniffing, Laurel took a step back so she could see her daughter. "Mommy's okay, baby." She forced a smile.

"Go sit with her," Wes encouraged Laurel. "Drink your coffee while I get her drink and clean up." To his surprise, Laurel nodded her agreement and went to sit by their daughter.

A few minutes later, Wes handed Sarah-Jane her cup before joining them at the round table.

"I'm sorry I went off on you like that." Laurel wrapped her fingers around her cup. "You didn't deserve it."

"No, but I also know you didn't mean it, so we're good. However, I have something I need to tell you."

Straightening, she lifted her cup. "Go ahead. I doubt it could be anything worse."

"I took a picture of Jimmy's ID yesterday and sent it to a friend of mine who ran a background check."

Her suddenly wide eyes searched his. "And?"

"From all appearances, Jimmy Donovan is a stand-up guy. He owns a drilling business out in the Permian Basin, and his only run-in with the law was over thirty years ago, when he served six months for possession with intent to distribute a controlled substance."

Nodding, she leaned back in her chair. "I guess he was telling the truth, then. At least about that part."

Did Wes dare press her to let him in? To tell him about what she'd learned yesterday?

He took a deep breath. "What else did he have to say?"

Over the next several minutes, Laurel opened up, revealing her grandmother's offer to help Jimmy when he got out of jail and how his letters to her mother were not only returned but followed by divorce papers.

"I feel like I've been lied to all my life. I can't believe my grandmother would deliberately try to keep my parents apart. I thought she was the only person I could trust. Now it appears she was simply the puppeteer manipulating everyone else for the outcome she wanted."

While a part of him wanted to agree, he said, "I'm sure she had her reasons. Probably thought she was protecting you and your mother."

"By tearing apart my family?" She huffed. "What kind of person does that?"

Of course, this was assuming Jimmy was telling the truth. But he also could have been trying to deflect responsibility. "Does Jimmy blame her?"

Laurel thought for moment, emptied the last of her coffee. "If he does, he didn't say it. He simply laid out what I assume are facts."

Wes had to give the guy credit for that.

"I don't understand why my grandmother would return those letters without ever giving them to my mother."

"I'm sorry to say, that's something you'll probably never know."

Her gaze drifted to Sarah-Jane. "Are you all finished, baby?"

The child waved her hands in the air.

Laurel chuckled. "Good girl."

Wes stood and went into the kitchen to dampen a paper towel, then came back to wipe off his daughter's hands and face. When he was finished, he lifted Sarah-Jane out of her chair and set her on her feet. She promptly headed into the living room.

"He said he's dying, Wes."

He faced Laurel.

Standing, she continued. "That's why he wanted to find me."

"Wow." He shoved a hand through his hair. "How do you feel about that?"

"That's just it—I don't know how I feel. I mean, I thought I knew everything. I thought he walked out on me and my mother. I thought he rejected me. Now it appears that wasn't the case at all."

"Do you plan to talk to him again?"

"I don't know. He said he's staying at the Bliss Inn for a few days, in case I wanted to talk, and he gave me his number. But… I just don't know."

"I understand your hesitation. However, you might want to ask yourself this. How are you going to feel if you don't? Especially since you know he's dying."

"I'll probably regret it. But I'm not sure I want to expose Sarah-Jane to him. At least not yet. Not until I'm sure."

"I'm in complete agreement with you there. Why don't you ask him to meet you for lunch somewhere so there will be other people around? I mean, you're already taking Sarah-Jane to the sitter. And if you want me to go with you, I will."

She blinked at him. "You'd do that?"

At this moment, there wasn't a whole lot he wouldn't do for her. He cupped her cheek. "In a heartbeat."

She pulled away then and smiled. "I appreciate that." Drawing in a long breath, she continued, "But I'm afraid this is something I'm going to tackle alone."

He couldn't say that he blamed her. Still, "In that case, I'm only a phone call away if you need me."

Laurel opted to meet Jimmy at Rae's Fresh Start Café. Given how difficult their conversation was likely to be, Laurel decided it might encourage her, at least, to have it in familiar territory. Not that her porch hadn't been familiar. She knew what she was getting into today, though. Or hoped so, anyway. She wasn't sure she could handle any more bombshells.

She arrived early so she could inform Rae as to what was going on and then snagged a table near the back, where they weren't as likely to be interrupted every time someone walked in the door. Finally, at 11:44 a.m., one minute before their designated meeting time, Jimmy Donovan walked into the restaurant. He was a handsome man and carried himself well. No wonder her mother had fallen for him.

But there was something else about him. A sadness. Not just because of the current situation or his illness, but a deep-rooted ache. The kind that comes from a broken heart.

Shaking off the notion, and as much of her sympathy as she could manage, she stood so he could see her.

His smile grew wide when he did, albeit a tad tremulous. Moments later, he was beside her. Hands buried in the pockets of his jeans, he said, "I was kinda surprised to hear from you."

"A sleepless night left me with a lot of questions. Questions I'm hoping you can answer for me."

"I'll do my best."

She motioned for him to sit down as she eased into her chair once again. Rae promptly brought them each water and a menu. After small talk and placing their orders, Laurel was ready to dive in.

Arms crossed, she rested them on the wooden tabletop. "Tell me about my mother. What was she like?"

A faraway look glimmered in his eyes. "She was the epitome of vivacious. Fun, full of energy, always saw the best in everyone and everything. Including me." He shifted in his seat. "I'll never forget the first time I saw her. It was at a high school football game. She was a cheerleader, you know. Had that cute little skirt and sweater." His smile faded slightly, and he looked at Laurel. "She was the only person who ever believed in me, and I was determined to prove myself worthy. I ended up letting her down instead."

That last little tidbit had tears prickling Laurel's eyes, but she managed to blink them away. Still, the way he talked about her mother… He really had loved her. Perhaps still did.

"The investigator told me she'd passed on. How did she die?"

Fingering the wrapper on her unopened straw, Laurel said, "Drugs." A sigh escaped. "I was ten, so my memories of her are vague. I just remember that she was always leaving. I'd stay with my grandmother while Mom ran off with guy after guy. Then she'd come back a few weeks later, usually brokenhearted, promising that things were going to be different. Then, before I knew it, she'd be gone again."

Jimmy's countenance grew distressed. "And all these years I just assumed she'd found love again."

"I think she kept looking, she just never found it."

A myriad of conversations, none of them intelligible, swirled through the sudden silence.

Jimmy's Adam's apple bobbed up and down rapidly, and he seemed to struggle for composure. "I guess my leaving really messed her up."

"Perhaps. However, after taking in everything you told me, and looking at those letters, seeing my grandmother's handwriting on the envelopes, I'm starting to get the feeling Mom never knew the reason *why* you left. Like me, I think she thought you'd abandoned us. And as much as it pains me to say this, I think that's what my grandmother wanted us to believe."

"I'm so sorry Laurel. I let pride get the best of me—" a tear spilled onto his cheek "—and ended up hurting the two people I love most in this world."

Laurel's vision blurred. How she had dreamed of hearing her father say he loved her. That he hadn't abandoned her. Or rejected her. He'd wanted her.

"There wasn't a day that's gone by I didn't send up a prayer for you."

Reaching for her napkin, a move that sent her silverware clanging against the table, she stared at him. "You did?" She dabbed her eyes.

"I couldn't be there to watch over you, so I asked the Lord to do it in my stead."

Through tears, she said, "You have no idea how much I want to believe that."

"I understand." Straightening, he sucked in a breath. "Trust is something that needs to be earned. But I intend to use whatever time I've got left to do just that."

Here she was, in the middle of a restaurant, and the tears simply wouldn't stop. This would not do. "I'm sorry—" she sniffed "—but we're going to have to change the subject before I turn into a bawling heap."

He chuckled.

She blew her nose. "Um, so you own a drilling company?"

His brow lifted. "Sounds like you've done some research."

"Actually, Wes did." She reached for her water. "He had a friend run a background check."

"Can't say as I blame him. He was trying to protect you, like a good husband should."

"Well, he's retired military, if that tells you anything. And..." Setting her cup back down without ever having taken a drink, she wondered if she should tell him. Yesterday she hadn't wanted Jimmy to know any details about her life. But then, she'd also believed he was a fraud, someone who only wanted something from her. Now, though, she actually believed he was her father and the reasons behind his sudden appearance were sincere.

Meeting his gaze once again, she said, "Wes is not my husband."

"Oh." Jimmy looked surprised. "I just assumed."

"It's a rather complicated situation." Out of the corner of her eye, Laurel saw Rae approach.

"All right, I've got your beef tips with noodles." Rae set the plate in front of Laurel then handed the other plate to Jimmy. "And chicken fried steak for the gentleman."

"Thank you, young lady."

"Can I get you anything else?" Rae said those same words to everyone in her restaurant. But the look she sent Laurel said she was ready to provide a means of escape if Laurel needed it.

"No." Laurel winked. "I think we're good."

A smile lit Rae's blue eyes. "Glad to hear it." She patted Laurel's shoulder. "Just holler if you need me."

Laurel was surprised when Jimmy asked if he could say grace. Then, over their meal, Laurel explained her and Wes's relationship. What little of it she understood, anyway.

"It's obvious he cares about you very much." Jimmy shoved another bite of steak into his mouth.

She thought about the feel of Wes's hand touching

her face. Oh, how she'd wanted to lean into it. To feel his embrace once again.

Shrugging, she nabbed a forkful of noodles. "He's an honorable man, and I happen to be the mother of his child."

"I saw firsthand how fiercely protective he was of you." Knife in one hand, fork in the other, he cut another piece of meat.

"He was protecting his daughter."

Jimmy glanced up at her. "Don't kid yourself, Laurel."

She wasn't kidding herself—she was protecting her heart. Her feelings for Wes had begun to shift, moving into unfamiliar and terrifying territory. Believing that his feelings were only because of Sarah-Jane was what Laurel needed to keep her from getting her hopes up.

"Well, it doesn't really matter, anyway, because Wes is leaving soon."

Jimmy's brow lifted in question.

"He's going to Iraq for a year to work with Servant's Heart."

"I've heard of them. However, a year's not that long, then he'll be back."

She paused, her fork in midair. "I'm not trying to be hurtful, but the concept of coming back isn't something I can easily wrap my head around."

He frowned, nodding. "Laurel, your grandmother loved you. I'm sure she thought she was doing the right thing by you. She took very good care of you. Left you her entire estate, from what I hear."

"Yes, but she took away the only thing I ever really wanted."

Chapter Thirteen

Wes needed to stop thinking about Laurel. Ever since that night they had dinner with Irma and Joyce, his resolve to steer clear of romantic relationships had seemed to be fading fast when it came to her. Perhaps all that talk about weddings had gotten to him.

Whatever the case, he needed to get a grip. Just because he and Laurel shared a daughter didn't mean that they were destined to be together. Sure, he cared about her and wanted what was best for her. But Wes wasn't the best. He'd failed his parents. He couldn't bear it if he failed Laurel, too.

By the grace of God, he'd managed to keep himself in check when she'd stopped by Irma's a little over an hour ago to let him know how things had gone with Jimmy. She seemed to be getting closer to accepting that the man was, indeed, her father, which was something Wes couldn't argue with based on everything she'd told him.

Pulling the front door closed at Irma's just after three, he twisted the key in the dead bolt before heading toward his truck. He'd accomplished everything on his list today—added the subfloor to the bathroom, removed the remaining vinyl and then did the drywall repair on the family room ceiling. He supposed he should start thinking about what he was going to say at the men's prayer breakfast tomorrow. He could make a list of the details he wanted to be sure to touch on.

But first, he owed his sister some attention. He'd been spending so much time with Laurel and Sarah-Jane that Rae had become relegated to a back burner, and that wasn't fair. Not after all she'd done for him. At least he'd managed to get in most of the painting she'd wanted done.

Rae was in her newly opened-up kitchen, folding laundry at the table when he arrived.

"You're home early." She set a towel on the table. "Did you accomplish much?"

"There's no longer a gaping hole in Irma's family room, if that tells you anything." He set his tool bag on the wooden floor, in the corner by the table, then headed to the sink to wash up.

"Sounds like progress." Adding another towel to the growing stack, she said, "By the way, I just got off the phone with Laurel. We're going to dinner with her and Sarah-Jane tonight." She grabbed another towel from the basket on the chair. "I'm craving Mexican and some time with my niece, so I figured I may as well kill two birds with one stone. And since you've been spending all of your time with them anyway..."

He turned the hot water on and squirted soap onto his hands. Just when he'd decided he should take a break from Laurel. Then again, a meal with his sister at a restaurant wasn't the same as the two of them and Sarah-Jane feeling like a family at Laurel's house.

After working up a lather, he scrubbed his hands and forearms.

Behind him, his sister continued. "How are things going between you and Laurel, anyway?"

He cringed, not wanting to talk about Laurel. "We're adjusting." He moved his arms back and forth beneath the stream of water, hoping his sister wouldn't press the conversation.

"That's not what I mean, and you know it." Glancing over his shoulder, he saw a frustrated Rae set the final towel atop the stack. "Is there any chance the two of you could, you know, have a future together?"

As if he deserved a future with Laurel or anybody else. Rae knew better. He'd cost their parents their lives. That was why he had to forfeit his.

"Not with me leaving soon." Turning off the water with his elbow, he reached for the dish towel on the counter.

"But you'll be back." Rae was not about to let this go. "Besides, I've seen the way you two look at each other."

Hands clean and dry, he threw the towel back onto the counter. "We share a child, Rae. Of course we're going to have a mutual respect for one another."

Skepticism narrowed her blue eyes. "Mutual respect, huh?" Crossing her arms over her chest, she continued to watch him.

He retrieved a glass from the cupboard. "Don't do this to me, Rae. You know where I stand when it comes to relationships."

"Then how do you explain Sarah-Jane?"

Reaching for the handle on the fridge, he froze. He hated it when she was right. Because he still couldn't understand how he'd allowed that night to happen.

He yanked open the door and filled his glass with some iced tea without saying a word. Then he slammed the door closed, went into the living room and dropped onto the leather couch, all without so much as a glance toward his sister. He could only hope she'd take a hint.

Instead, she crossed the room and sat down beside him, setting a hand on his knee. "You're a good man, Wesley. A man who's spent his entire adult life serving others. I know you feel as though you deserve to be punished for what happened to Dad and Mom, but I think your sentence has been served."

He watched her out of the corner of his eye. "Don't tell me you've never blamed me, Rae. I mean, look at all you gave up."

She stared at him. "Not once. I may not have liked it. I certainly didn't understand why, but I never blamed you or anyone else for their accident. Because that's just what it was, an accident." With a final pat, she walked away. "I saw Laurel's father today."

His sister knew him well and understood he was done discussing the previous topic. Of course, not without having her own say. "And?"

"She introduced him on their way out." Returning to the table, she began folding a pile of clothes.

"Did she refer to him as her father?" Grateful for the reprieve, he stretched an arm across the back of the sofa.

"No, she called him Jimmy, but I have no doubt that he is her father. She looks a lot like him. Same eyes, same smile."

He took a sip of his tea, the cold liquid soothing his suddenly parched throat. "Any other observations?"

"No, I tried to leave them alone. They were pretty deep in conversation. Though I did notice a few tears from both of them." She dropped the shirt she'd just picked up. "Oh, I almost forgot." Moving to the kitchen counter, she retrieved a large envelope. "A package came for you from Servant's Heart." She started toward him.

He leaned forward to deposit his cup on the coffee table with one hand while intercepting the envelope with the other. "Must be the paperwork they told me about." After digging his pocketknife from his jeans, he sliced open the top.

Pulling out the forms, he sifted through them. They wanted him to list a beneficiary, which wasn't much different from serving overseas with the military. In the past, he'd always listed Rae. But that was before Sarah-Jane.

"You look awful serious over there." Rae continued to fold. "What's in the packet?"

"The usual stuff." He lifted his head to look at her. "What should I do about the beneficiary this time?"

"What's your first instinct?"

"Laurel."

Rae shot him a smile and a thumbs-up. "I was hoping you'd say that."

"But I've always named you."

"And you think you'll be hurting my feelings." She shook her head. "Wesley, you know I don't need the money." Rae had gotten the last laugh when the judge ordered her ex-husband to pay her for her half of the car dealership they'd owned together, allowing Rae to walk away with a tidy chunk of change. "Besides, I'm not raising your child. If anything happens to you, the money should go to Laurel."

Staring at the paperwork in his lap, his new job suddenly became more real. He'd be leaving in just a little over a week. He was used to leaving, except things had changed. This time he'd be leaving someone besides Rae. Truth be told, two very important someones—

Laurel and Sarah-Jane. Could he do that? Not that he had a choice. He was committed. If only he'd known about Sarah-Jane before he signed his contract.

He shoved a hand through his hair. This could be his toughest assignment yet.

Laurel was glad when Rae had called and suggested they do dinner. She hadn't had much time with her friends since Wes came to town. And with her father showing up, well, she could really use a friend about now. There were so many thoughts tumbling through her head that it was difficult to sort them all out. Perhaps a change of scenery and a listening ear would help. Even if Wes was going to be there, too.

She pulled into the already full parking lot of La Familia just as Rae and Wes were exiting his truck. Rae hurried over and hugged Laurel as she got out while Wes unhooked Sarah-Jane from her car seat. Moments later, they all made their way inside the colorful eatery, where they were greeted with the enticing aromas of fresh-made tortillas, sizzling meat and spices.

Laurel's mouth watered in anticipation.

Despite the busy Friday-night crowd, they were seated right away. Something Laurel was more than grateful for, because she was starving. With so many tears over lunch, she'd found her appetite waning. Now, it was back with a vengeance, along with a sudden craving for Mexican food.

While Wes studied his menu, Laurel had already settled on the cheese enchiladas, so she simply sat back and took in the busyness of the place. Waiters and waitresses scurrying back and forth with large trays laden with food, patrons talking and laughing, and Rae playing peekaboo with Sarah-Jane, making the child giggle.

Grabbing a tortilla chip from the bowl on the table, she scooped up a fair amount of salsa, her gaze drifting toward the door. Somehow, beyond the throng of waiting people, she spotted Jimmy Donovan. He was alone, of course, and something about that bothered her.

She glanced toward her daughter. Did she dare invite him to join them? Would Wes be okay with that? After all, they had yet to expose Sarah-Jane to the man. But then, what if he saw them?

As she continued to stare, Wes nudged her elbow. "Do you want to ask him to come sit with us?"

Her gaze shifted to the man beside her. "I don't know. What about Sarah-Jane?"

Rae leaned across the table. "What are y'all whispering about?"

"My father is here." Only after the words left her mouth did Laurel realize that she'd referred to him as her father instead of Jimmy. Perhaps this was the beginning of acceptance.

"Why don't you invite him to join us, then?" Rae made it sound so simple. "That is, unless you don't want to."

"It's not that. It's just that he hasn't met Sarah-Jane yet."

Rae briefly glanced over her shoulder in the direction Wes and Rae had been looking. "Do you think he poses any sort of threat to her?"

"No. It's just all so…new."

"Hmm… Kind of like when Wes showed up, huh?" Rae reached for a tortilla chip. "Look on the bright side—you're surrounded by friends." She motioned between herself and Wes.

Laurel saw Rae's point, though she still found herself

looking to Wes for guidance. After all, he was Sarah-Jane's father.

He smiled. "Go ask him. I'll have the waiter bring another setup and menu."

Standing, Laurel took in a deep breath and crossed the terra-cotta pavers to where Jimmy waited, aware that this would likely signal a change in their relationship.

"Jimmy?"

He looked up at her with a smile she'd seen a thousand times on Sarah-Jane.

"I didn't expect to see you here."

"I'm with Wes, my best friend, Rae, and Sarah-Jane. My daughter. Would you care to join us?"

As he stood, his smile became more tremulous. "Aw, I'd hate to intrude."

"You're not intruding. You're invited." It surprised her when she realized that she actually meant it.

"In that case, I'd be honored."

Amid the sounds of mariachi music, they returned to the table, where Wes formally introduced himself and Rae.

"And this is Sarah-Jane." A sense of pride washed over Laurel. "Your granddaughter."

He crouched beside the high chair, his gray-green eyes filled with wonder. "Hello, Sarah-Jane. You sure are a cute little thing. Just look at those pretty blue eyes."

"She has her father to thank for those," said Laurel.

"Though I don't think anyone has ever said mine are pretty." Wes bit into another chip.

"At least not since you were little," injected Rae.

Once they sat down, the conversation remained casual, just as Rae had suggested. And it was comforting to have Rae and Wes asking Jimmy questions about himself, giving Laurel more insight into the man she had so much to learn about. Like the fact that he'd never remarried. Laurel wasn't sure what to read into that, but given their conversation earlier today, it was obvious he had loved her mother very much. And from what she knew about her mother, she suspected the feeling was mutual.

When the waiter brought the check, Jimmy insisted on picking up the tab. "Y'all made me feel welcome, and I appreciate that."

Rae and Jimmy fussed over Sarah-Jane as they exited the restaurant into the steamy night air.

Moving into the parking lot, Laurel tugged Wes aside. "Do you think it would be okay to invite him over to the house for a little bit? Maybe let him see Sarah-Jane in her element. Of course, she'll be going to bed soon, so—"

"Laurel." With a grin that made his blue eyes sparkle, Wes reached for her arm. "He's your father. It's fine."

Her gaze darted to the older man, uncertainty still lingering. "Would you—?"

"Rae and I will be happy to join you."

She couldn't help smiling. It seemed Wes knew her too well.

She caught up to her father. "Jimmy?"

He turned.

"Would you like to—"

His face suddenly went ashen, his expression going blank.

She stretched out a hand, attempting to reach for him. "Jimmy, are you o—"

But before she could get the words out, he collapsed.

"Jimmy!" She dropped to her knees.

"What happened?" Wes was at her side, rolling the man onto his back.

"I don't know. The color drained from his face, then he went down." She gasped when she saw the blood oozing from a gash on his forehead. *God, please don't let my father die now. I just found him. Please.*

Tears stung the backs of her eyes as Wes checked Jimmy's pulse.

"Jimmy?" He continued to evaluate the man. "Can you hear me?" He looked at Laurel. "Do you have a rag or anything else in the diaper bag we can use for the bleeding?"

Moving the strap off her shoulder, Laurel saw Rae looking on, bouncing a blessedly oblivious Sarah-Jane.

"The hospital is right up the street, if you need it," said Rae. "It'd probably be quicker to take him than wait on an ambulance."

Hospital? Ambulance? Laurel hastily unzipped the main compartment of her bag and dug through it until she came up with an old cloth bib. "Here." She thrust it toward Wes as her father began to rouse. "Thank You, God." She fell back on her flip-flop-covered heels, grateful for Wes's combat service. She could trust him to take care of her father just as well as any EMT.

"Jimmy?" Wes waited for the man to make eye contact. "I'm going to help you into my truck and take you to the hospital, all right?"

Thankfully, her father nodded his agreement.

Minutes later, Wes, Jimmy and Laurel were on their way to the hospital, while Rae took Sarah-Jane home in Laurel's SUV. Laurel sat in the back seat with Jimmy, holding the bib to his forehead and praying like never before. She couldn't lose him. Not with everything she'd learned today. He loved her, and he'd always wanted her. She squeezed her eyes shut. *God, please.*

When they arrived at the emergency room, the aides put Jimmy on a gurney and promptly whisked him away.

"Are you all related to this man?" A young woman wearing bright pink scrubs looked from Laurel to Wes and back again.

"He's my father," Laurel managed to eke out.

Fearful, she collapsed into a nearby chair, the antiseptic smells threatening to overwhelm her. Wes joined her, reaching for her hand. Strange how she was so used to taking care of herself, and yet tonight, she appreciated Wes's take-charge attitude. And the strength of his touch was what she needed right now.

After what felt like an eternity, Laurel and Wes were accompanied to her father's exam room, where the doctor informed them that it was likely Jimmy's elevated blood pressure that caused him to black out.

"Coupled with the head wound, I'd like to go ahead and keep him overnight for observation," the doctor continued.

The news came as a relief to Laurel. The thought of her father going back to a hotel room all alone made her nervous.

She and Wes remained at the hospital until her father was settled into his room. Then they bade him goodnight with a promise from Laurel that she'd be by in the morning.

Once back at Laurel's place, they relayed all of the information to Rae, then she excused herself and went on out to Wes's truck.

Alone, Laurel reached for Wes's hand. "Thank you

for staying with me. Without you, I'm pretty sure I would have fallen apart."

"Nah, you're a strong woman."

"I like to think so, but not tonight. You were my rock."

His gaze searched hers for the longest time, and she thought—perhaps even hoped—that he was going to kiss her. Instead, he took a step back and said, "Rae's waiting on me."

Turning away, she cleared her throat, doing her best to ignore the disappointment sifting through her. "Yes, you should go." Because while she'd allowed herself to get caught up in the moment, thinking Wes might actually be interested in her romantically, she now realized that wasn't the case. She and Wes were friends and nothing more. And, somehow, Laurel would have to find a way to live with that.

Chapter Fourteen

After all that scolding Wes had done yesterday, reminding himself why he should stay away from Laurel, he'd almost kissed her. What had gotten into him?

Laurel had. She'd gotten to him in a way no other woman ever had. Every time they were together, he found himself wanting things he couldn't have. Things he didn't deserve.

His frustration was still in full force when he pulled up to the church Saturday morning, and he found himself wondering why he'd even agreed to attend the men's prayer breakfast. Yes, he was heading into the mission field, but he wasn't your average missionary. He was a hands-on worker-bee kind of guy, which was why Servant's Heart had hired him to manage their shelter construction program. He not only loved what he did, he was good at it. But standing in front of a bunch of strangers and talking about his faith wasn't his style.

Yet, despite his misgivings, he still found himself in the church's fellowship hall, gathered around a long table with several men he didn't know. His belly full of some of the finest breakfast tacos he'd ever had, he talked about his upcoming venture. At least they hadn't asked him to stand.

"From what I hear, the entire country of Iraq was left in ruins." An older gentleman who looked every bit a rancher with tanned skin and a full head of white hair gripped a foam coffee cup opposite Wes.

"You may be right, sir." Under the glow of bright white LED lights, he continued, "I can personally attest to the fact that the war in Iraq destroyed many homes, neighborhoods and villages. Our rebuilding efforts are a way of showing Christ's love to the Iraqi people in a tangible manner."

The same man lifted a brow. "Did you serve in Iraq?"

"Yes, sir."

"Which branch of the service were you in?" a man about Wes's age piped up at the far end of the table.

"Navy."

"My grandson is in the navy." Another older gentleman smiled proudly.

"How long were you in?" the stocky fellow next to Wes asked.

"I was a Seabee for twenty years before retiring a couple of years ago."

"You must have joined quite young, then." The pastor watched him curiously.

"Right out of high school."

Eyeing the round black clock on the wall, the pastor said, "Fellas, this has been a great discussion." He faced Wes. "Wes, we'll keep you in our prayers. And, if you have an opportunity, drop us an email and let us know how things are going and how we can specifically pray for you during your time in Iraq."

Given the state of his attitude when he'd walked into

the church earlier, Wes was humbled. "I will do that, sir. Thank you."

After the pastor closed with a word of prayer, chairs scraped across the linoleum floor as the men stood, gathering their trash. Most paused to shake Wes's hand and thank him for his service on their way out the door.

"I'll have to add my thanks once again." With everyone else gone, the pastor gathered the sugar, creamer and a stack of foam cups from beside the coffeepot that sat on a small table set off to one side. "I know that was short notice, so I appreciate you taking the time to come."

Wes grabbed the empty box that once held the tacos and the partial box of doughnuts and followed the pastor into the kitchen. "I'll admit that I was a little apprehensive at first. But I actually enjoyed it."

"I'm glad to hear that." The older man deposited his armload on the long center island, and Wes did the same. "So, what made you decide to become a Seabee?"

To atone for my parents' deaths was the first thing that came to Wes's mind.

"I knew I wanted to serve in the military. When I went to see the recruiter, he talked about the Seabees, and I got really pumped. I had no idea there was such a thing. My dad and I used to build things all the time and I really enjoyed it, so it seemed like a natural fit." He lifted a shoulder. "Besides, I needed to give Rae her life back."

When the pastor sent him a confused look, Wes went on. "Our parents died when I was still in high school. Rae put college on hold to finish raising me. Something I know I didn't deserve."

"Why do you say that?"

Contemplating the man beside him, Wes found himself in a quandary. He could easily come up with some offhanded remark about being a teenager that might appease the guy's curiosity, or he could tell him the truth.

Not so different from the dilemma Laurel had faced last Sunday when she introduced Wes as Rae's brother. Her half-truth had not only hurt Wes, it had left her riddled with guilt. And guilt was something Wes was all too acquainted with.

Resting a hand atop the counter, he said, "I'm the reason my parents are dead." His words were blunt, he knew that, yet Pastor Kleinschmidt didn't even flinch.

Eyed narrowed, the pastor studied him. "You really believe that?"

"I do."

Lines formed on the man's brow as he continued to watch Wes. "How did they die?"

"Car crash."

"Were you driving?"

"No."

"Then how could it be your fault?"

"Because they were coming to pick me up from camp." Crossing his arms, he drew in a long breath and leaned his backside against the counter. "I was sixteen. Me and this other kid had gotten into a fight, so they called our parents to come and get us." He found himself staring at the dropped ceiling, unable to look the pastor in the eye. "It was raining really hard that night. They shouldn't have been out on the roads. But they were. Because of me." Mustering his courage, he met the pastor's concerned gaze. "Just another in a long line of bad choices I've made in my life. Except the impact of that one was far-reaching."

The pastor remained silent for a moment, as though searching for the right words. "Wes, the Bible says,

'When I was a child, I thought as a child: but when I became a man, I put away childish things.' As a sixteen-year-old boy, you convinced yourself that you alone were responsible for your parents' deaths, when nothing could be further from the truth."

Wes struggled to grasp what the pastor was trying to say. If he hadn't gotten into that fight, his parents wouldn't have been out in that storm. Dad wouldn't have lost control of the car.

"Did you cause the storm that night, Wes?"

"Of course, not. Only God can do that."

"That's right." The pastor's lips tilted into a half smile as he leaned against the opposite counter. "Wes, sometimes God allows things to happen that our feeble minds simply cannot understand. But God is still in control. And He has a plan and purpose for each of us."

Wes let the pastor's words rumble around his brain for a minute. "I understand what you're saying up here." He tapped the side of his head. "It's in here—" he pointed to his heart "—where I struggle."

"You can't make sense of your parents' deaths, so it's easier to blame yourself."

"Something like that, yeah."

"Then how about, instead of blaming yourself, you choose to trust that God was in control that night your parents died? That He still has a plan for you. And that Sarah-Jane, perhaps even Laurel, are part of that plan."

Why would he mention Laurel? Did the pastor know, could he see, how Wes felt about her? "It sounds too simple."

"Trusting means letting go, Wes. And I don't know about you, but for me, letting go is never easy."

When I became a man, I put away childish things.

Could he really do it? Could he let go of the belief that he'd caused his parents' deaths? After all these years.

God, I want to believe You're in control. Help me. Please.

He eyed the man across from him. "Pastor, will you pray with me?"

"I'd be happy to, Wes."

There was nothing special in the pastor's prayer. No big words, nothing fancy. Yet when Wes walked out of the church twenty minutes later, he felt lighter. It was as though the burden of his past, the one that had weighed him down for so many years, had been lifted from his shoulders. And as thoughts of Sarah-Jane and Laurel sifted into his mind, he began to wonder if, maybe, he might be worthy of a family, after all.

"I've put the paint for each room in that particular room." With Sarah-Jane in one arm and Paisley at her side, Laurel moved from Irma's entry hall into the bedroom Saturday morning, pointing toward the cans near the window. "Rollers, trays and drop cloths are in the family room, along with that blue painter's tape, if you need it."

"Darlin', you've got nothing to worry about." Even in paint clothes, which consisted of torn jeans, a tailored T-shirt and canvas sneakers, Paisley looked like a fashionista. "I've painted more rooms in my lifetime than many professionals."

"Paisley, I really appreciate you helping me out like this." Laurel was supposed to meet her friend and a couple of other women from the church to do the painting at Irma's today. But with Laurel's father in the hospital, she'd asked Paisley if she could take charge of the task in her stead.

"Look, it's not every day a girl finds her long-lost father." Her friend draped an arm around Laurel's shoulder and gave her a sideways hug. "He needs you, so I'm happy to help."

Laurel wasn't sure what she'd done to deserve such wonderful friends, but she was blessed to have them.

After going over everything, she loaded Sarah-Jane into her car seat and drove across town toward the hospital.

Glimpsing her daughter in the rearview mirror, she said, "How do you like that, Sarah-Jane? Only a few weeks ago, it was just us. Now you have a daddy and a grandpa." Not to mention Rae. Tears attempted to blur her vision, though she managed to thwart them. "You have a family, baby." And so did Laurel. After all these years of thinking he'd rejected her, she had a father.

Lord, please don't take him too soon. She wanted the opportunity to get to know Jimmy and make memories.

Under a cloudless sky, she continued on to the hospital. Since all indications were that Jimmy would be discharged today, she wanted to be there to take him back to his hotel to rest, and maybe spend a little time with him until she knew he was settled. Even if he wasn't discharged, she wanted to be there for him. Being in the hospital alone was just plain sad. Fortunately, when she'd had Sarah-Jane, she'd almost never been alone. It seemed either Rae, Christa or Paisley was always there with her, keeping her company, bringing her coffee, pastries and a big ol' basket full of snacks for her and booties, onesies, wipes and pacifiers for Sarah-Jane.

After parking, Laurel retrieved her daughter from the back seat. "Let's go see your grandpa." She supposed she'd have to ask him what he preferred to be called. Grandpa, Pawpaw, Granddaddy…

Holding Sarah-Jane, she made her way across the parking lot and through the automatic double doors at the front of the hospital, then continued down a series of hallways until she came to his room.

"Good morn—" She stopped just inside the doorway. The room was empty. Not only that, the light was off, and the adjustable bed was stripped, as though her father had never been there.

A nurse breezed past the door just then.

"Excuse me." Laurel stepped back into the hall.

The woman sporting short, slightly graying hair did a quick about-face. "Oh, hey, Laurel."

"Ginny, hey. It's good to see you."

"Look at this baby." Ginny, someone Laurel was acquainted with from church, cooed at Sarah-Jane. "She gets cuter every time I see her." Her attention returned to Laurel. "Is she walking yet?"

"Barely, but yes." She shifted Sarah-Jane to her other arm as an aide swept by, pushing a blood pressure cart. "Um, they moved my father, Jimmy Donovan, into this room last night. Can you tell me where he is now?"

"I didn't know he was your father." Ginny palmed her forehead. "Silly me, I didn't even make the connection. He was discharged a couple of hours ago."

"Discharged?" Laurel's heart squeezed. "Did someone pick him up?"

"I don't recall seeing anyone, unless they picked him up out front. Would you like me to see who escorted him out? Perhaps they could tell you more."

Who just walks out of a hospital? And why wouldn't he have called her? Or even waited, since she'd told him she'd see him in the morning. Unless he didn't want to see her.

"No, that won't be necessary. Thank you, Ginny."

The early May sun had turned hot by the time Laurel made it back to her vehicle. Sweat beaded her forehead. Maybe Jimmy had had someone drive him to get his truck. Then again, it wasn't like Bliss had any taxis. Still, he could have asked someone for a ride. Someone who wasn't his daughter.

She again loaded Sarah-Jane into her car seat. "I'm sorry, baby, but we need to find your grandfather."

A few minutes later, she pulled into the parking lot of La Familia. Jimmy's truck was no longer there.

The familiar ache of rejection threatened to overwhelm her. Tears pricked the backs of her eyes, and her throat tightened. He was gone. Without even saying goodbye.

Sucking in a deep breath, she continued over to the Bliss Inn, where she finally spotted his big white pickup truck, though her relief was merely replaced by angst.

She pulled into the mostly empty parking lot of the '50s-era single-story motel that had recently been renovated and eased into the space beside his truck, which was parked right in front of his door. With her vehicle still running, she said, "I'll be right back, Sarah-Jane." She locked the doors via the keypad on the driver's door before marching to Jimmy's door a few feet away.

She knocked three times and waited long enough to feel the heat rising off the asphalt. Was he even in there? What if something had happened? What if he'd passed out again?

Noting the window boxes filled with red and purple petunias, she gave three more emphatic knocks. "Jimmy?"

Panic and grief battled for her attention. But after a few minutes, she realized she'd done all she could.

Slowly, she started for her SUV, but she stopped when she heard something behind her.

"Laurel?"

Turning, she saw Jimmy standing in the doorway, wearing a T-shirt and a pair of basketball shorts. He ran a hand through his disheveled gray hair.

"I'm sorry, Laurel. I was asleep."

As much as she hated that she'd woke him— "Why didn't you let me know they released you? That you were coming back here?"

"I'm sorry. I guess I was sleep deprived. Those hospital folk were in and out of my room all night long, so as soon as they told me I could go, I did."

After sneaking a peek at Sarah-Jane, Laurel crossed her arms over her chest. "How did you get to your truck?"

"I walked."

If someone were to take her blood pressure right now, she was pretty sure it'd be off the charts.

With the hum of her car's engine echoing around her, she lowered her arms and stepped toward him. "*You walked?* After collapsing and hitting your head, you decided to walk. Seriously? Why didn't you call me?"

"It was early, and I didn't want to bother you. Especially after you were there so late last night."

"Bother me? As if thinking you'd run out on me again didn't bother me?" She knew she shouldn't have said it, but it was out there now.

He looked distressed. "Oh, Laurel, I never expected you'd feel that way. I would never do anything to hurt you."

"Well, you did. So, obviously we're going to have to set some ground rules here."

Still standing on the carpet just inside the door, he

shifted from one bare foot to the next. "Ground rules? Does this mean you're willing to have a relationship with me?"

A sense of relief washed over her. "You're my dad. Of course I want a relationship. I also want to know all about this congestive heart failure thing. Because now that I've found you, I plan to do everything in my power to see to it you're around for as long as possible."

Chapter Fifteen

Wes found himself looking out of Irma's front windows more frequently Monday morning, anticipating Laurel's arrival. Aside from the fact that they'd be finishing the painting in the family room and laying the tile in the bathroom, he wanted to see Laurel. To be with her, talk to her, see her beautiful smile. All too soon, he wouldn't have that luxury for twelve long months. And he wanted to know everything about her, the same way she wanted to know about Jimmy.

Her father had felt good enough to accompany them to church yesterday, then they'd all gone to Laurel's along with Rae for a lunch of smoked brisket, beans, coleslaw and potato salad from a local barbecue joint. The whole lot of them had spent the entire afternoon talking and playing with Sarah-Jane, reminding Wes of when he was a kid and he, Rae and their parents would go off on adventures or simply hang out.

Strange that he hadn't thought about that in years. With his parents gone, it was too painful. Now, he suddenly found himself longing for more days like that—days with Laurel and Sarah-Jane. But as the pastor had said, Wes would have to trust God's plan. He just wished that plan didn't involve him moving to the other side of the world.

Perhaps he should contact Eddie. Tell him what was going on. Maybe something else could be arranged.

No. Wes had made a commitment. Not only to his friend, but he'd signed a contract with the organization. Even if they could place him somewhere else, it wouldn't be in Bliss.

Returning to the family room, he picked up the roller he'd attached to an extension pole, dipped it into the five-gallon bucket that held the bright white paint and started his second coat on the ceiling. Paisley and the other ladies had made a big dent in the painting Saturday, finishing Irma's bedroom as well as the upstairs bath. Today he and Laurel would knock out the family room, allowing them to start moving stuff back into the space tomorrow.

Okay, so it was Laurel who was supposed to do the painting while he tackled the tile upstairs. But how could he talk with her if she was down here and he was up there? And if he helped her, this room would be finished faster, then, maybe, she could assist him with the tile, or at least keep him company.

It was strange how quickly his thoughts on a relationship with Laurel had changed. No longer was he fighting the feelings that always seemed to be there, no matter how much he tried to ignore them, which made him glad he'd opened up to Pastor Kleinschmidt. Even if it had been inadvertently, the man had hit the nail on the head. Wes couldn't make sense of what happened to his parents, so he blamed himself and did whatever he could to atone for his actions.

The front door opened then, and a wave of expectation swelled within him.

"Wes?" Just the sound of Laurel's voice made him smile.

"In here."

"Wow." Clad in denim shorts and a T-shirt, she stared at the ceiling. "That thing must have been really dingy, because it's so much brighter in here already."

He lowered the pole. "It had definitely yellowed with time."

She watched as he loaded more paint onto the roller. "Can I do some?"

"I've been trying to get this done so you can tackle the walls."

"I know." Her grin turned silly. "But this looks like fun."

"Fun?" He passed the pole to her. "In that case, be my guest."

Her gray-green eyes sparkled with mirth, like a child trying something new.

"Be sure to take off the excess paint."

She did as he instructed, then lifted the pole over her head and began moving the roller forward then back.

"Careful not to apply too much—"

A blot of paint dripped from the roller just then, hitting her on the cheek.

"Oh!" She promptly lowered the pole, which he intercepted, directing it back into the bucket.

"Pressure." He bit back a chuckle.

"Now you tell me." Laughing, she wiped a finger over the paint, but only succeeded in spreading it across her face.

"Let me help you." He pulled a rag from his back pocket. "At least it didn't get in your hair or your eyes." Taking a step closer, he cupped her chin in one hand and began wiping her cheek with the other.

"They don't call me Grace for nothing." She puffed out a chortle but went still when her eyes met his.

He liked that she could laugh at herself. However, the sweet fragrance of her shampoo had his heart thundering against his ribs. Or, perhaps, it was their proximity. All he had to do was lower his head and their lips would meet. The taste of her kiss had lived in his memory for the past two years. What would she do if he kissed her now? Would she kiss him back or turn away?

"Laurel, I—"

A knock at the door had her stepping away. And the sudden pink in her cheeks left him wondering what was going through her head. Was she embarrassed or relieved?

"I'll get that." His voice sounded unusually raspy. Clearing his throat, he handed her the rag before making his way through the entry hall. Opening the door, he saw Laurel's father standing on the porch. "Jimmy, come on in."

"I know you're busy, Wes, and I'm sorry to interrupt you, but I need to talk to Laurel."

She was already approaching. "What is it? Are you okay?" Panic laced her tone, and after what happened Friday, Wes couldn't blame her.

"Everything is fine, Laurel. But something's come up and I need to get back to Midland right away. I didn't want to leave without saying goodbye, though."

Her expression went flat. "But I thought you were going to stay for a few more days?"

"I did, too, but there's a problem with one of my rigs, and I need to be there to address it. I promise, I'll come back to Bliss just as soon as I can. Maybe this weekend."

"What about your heart, though? All that traveling can't be good for you."

"I'll be fine." Closing the short span between them, Jimmy rested his hands on her shoulders. "I promise I'll pull over if anything seems amiss."

Laurel searched the man's green eyes for a moment, then took a step back, wrapping her arms around her middle. "Drive safe."

"I will. You've got my number. Don't hesitate to call. If you need me, if you just want to talk." He paused a moment before adding, "I love you, Laurel."

Her quick nod said everything Wes needed to know. She hadn't just pulled away from her father physically, she'd pulled away emotionally, afraid of being let down again.

Jimmy turned his attention to Wes then and held out a hand. "It's been nice to meet you, Wes. If I don't see you before you leave, you take care of yourself."

"You, too, Jimmy."

Still hugging herself, Laurel made her way back into the family room the moment Jimmy closed the door.

Wes wished he could make her see that goodbye didn't mean forever. That what happened all those years ago with her parents was not the norm.

Except it was her norm. And now learning that her grandmother had manipulated the whole thing—tearing Laurel's family apart—had, in some ways, made things even worse.

Longing to comfort her, he followed her into the other room and found her staring out the window.

She must have heard him, because she said, "What if he doesn't come back?"

"He said he would." Moving across the canvas tarp, he stopped behind her. "And, if you'll recall, even the circumstances of him leaving the first time weren't as you believed."

"I know." In her head she might know, but had her heart had time to embrace the truth? "What if something happens to him?" She faced him now, and Wes saw the worry marring her brow. "You were there when he collapsed. What if that happens again?"

He let go a sigh. "We'll just have to pray and trust that God will bring him safely back to you."

"I don't know if he should be traveling so much. I mean, in his condition."

"He wants to be with you, Laurel." And Wes certainly couldn't fault him for that. "He wants to make up for all the time he missed."

She peered up at him, unshed tears shimmering in her pretty eyes. "I'm scared, Wes." Her bottom lip quivered.

Without a second thought, he wrapped his arms around her, tucking her head under his chin and holding her close as she cried.

Lord, please, bring Laurel's father back soon. Help her see that she is loved. Wanted. And not only by her father. Wes loved Laurel, too. The more time he spent with her, the more he wanted to build a life and a family with her. He wanted to protect her and shower her with all the love she deserved.

But all too soon, he would be leaving, too, which made convincing her his biggest challenge ever.

By Tuesday evening, Irma's place was finally starting to look like a home again. Paisley, the pastor's wife, Drenda, and a couple more ladies from the church had come by earlier to help Laurel with general cleanup and to put Irma's new bedroom together.

Since the wooden floor was still in good shape, they'd opted to add a large gray-and-white rug that encompassed the area under and around the antique bed—taking care to secure all of the edges—so Irma would have something soft to put her feet on when she got out of bed each morning. Then the sheer white curtains that covered the floor-to-ceiling windows were washed and rehung, while a couple of decorative shelves were added to one wall to display newly framed family photos, along with some trinkets Laurel had found shoved into one corner of the vintage oak dresser. Finally, they topped the room off with luxurious new bedding in a soothing pale cyan.

But what sent the room over the top and made it feel extra special was Irma's wedding dress. A dress form in the corner to the left of the windows proudly displayed the simple white satin gown with a chapel-length train, so it was one of the first things you saw when you entered the room. Laurel could hardly wait to see Irma's reaction.

Unfortunately, there was still much to do.

"Are you ready to see your daddy?" While the late-afternoon sun played peekaboo with the clouds, Laurel unhooked Sarah-Jane from her car seat in front of Irma's. Knowing Wes would be working late, Laurel had picked her daughter up from the sitter's then grabbed burgers, chicken nuggets and fries from Bubba's so they could spend a little time together before Sarah-Jane went to bed. With all he'd done for Laurel, it was the least she could do.

She'd never forget the feel of his arms around her yesterday. The way he'd held her close, trying his best to console her as she broke down. Yet, despite all of the reassuring Wes had offered her just prior, those old feelings of rejection refused to be ignored. So it came as a pleasant surprise when Jimmy called her last night to let her know that he'd made it home safely.

Lifting her daughter from the back seat, Laurel saw Wes coming toward her.

"Need a little help?" He rounded her vehicle.

"You want to take your daughter or your dinner?" She closed the back door.

"Let me see that munchkin." His tone was light and teasing as a smiling Sarah-Jane practically threw herself into his waiting arms. She was going to miss him when he left.

Laurel would, too.

Moving around to the passenger side, she grabbed the bag of food and the drink carrier and followed Wes inside.

"By the way, I finally took a look at the bedroom," he said as they moved into the parlor. "You ladies really transformed that space."

"I couldn't have done it without Paisley and Drenda, but it did come together nicely. I just hope Irma likes it."

They snaked their way through the parlor, past furniture and around boxes, until they reached the dining room table, where one end had been cleared.

"I'm sure she'll love it." Wes sat down in the high-backed chair at the head of the table with Sarah-Jane in his lap. "Are you ready for a French fry, Sarah-Jane?"

She happily clapped her hands as Laurel broke a couple into pieces and set them on a napkin in front of her daughter.

"Looks like we're going to have a busy day tomorrow." Laurel pulled out another bag of fries and passed them to Wes, along with his burger.

"Yeah, I sure hope all those guys who said they'd be

here at eight show up. Otherwise, I don't know how I'm going to get that tub back upstairs."

She laughed. "It's going to be strange not seeing it on the porch."

"I'm sure the neighbors will be pleased to see it gone, though."

Taking a seat beside Wes and her daughter, she cut Sarah-Jane's chicken nuggets with a plastic knife. "I still can't believe how quickly you got it done."

"Well, I wasn't juggling any other jobs." The man was too modest.

"No, just your sister and a daughter whom you'd never met before. Not to mention having to deal with her sometimes difficult mother."

He was about to take a bite of his burger but paused. "You're not difficult." The corners of his mouth lifted. "Challenging sometimes, but not difficult."

"Good." She slid the chicken in front of Sarah-Jane. "You needed a challenge."

When he'd finished chewing, he said, "From you, I welcome it." The playfulness glimmering in his blue eyes had her heart racing the same way it had yesterday when he was wiping the paint off her cheek.

Time to change the subject.

"When do you think Irma will be able to move back in?" She took a sip of her vanilla milkshake.

"Depends how long it's going to take you to get the rooms situated."

"I've got several people helping me tomorrow, including the guys who are supposed to move the tub. I'm counting on them to get those bookshelves back into the family room. Along with the sofa."

"If they're here at eight, they should be able to have everything moved by noon."

"That would be great. Then it's just merchandising the place and finding a more practical spot for all of those boxes." Picking up her burger, she motioned toward the parlor. "I definitely don't want them lining the walls in the bedroom again." She took a bite.

"What if I added some shelves in the closet?"

Once she'd finished chewing, she said, "You mean where there used to be more boxes?"

"Shelves would make better use of the space."

"True. Do you have time?"

"Sure. It won't take long. Worst case, I'll do it Thursday."

"Sounds like I'd better tell Irma she can move in Friday then."

"What were you thinking before?"

She picked up a fry. "I was hoping for Thursday, but I think I'm going to need the extra time to get everything situated the way I envision it."

"Friday it is, then." He popped a fry into his mouth. "And then you and I could go on a date Friday night to celebrate."

She felt her eyes widen. "A date?"

He grinned. "Yeah. A nice, leisurely dinner somewhere, just the two of us."

Shoving the fry in her mouth, she said, "What about Sarah-Jane?"

"I'm sure Rae will watch her."

With the air-conditioning whirring in the background, Laurel stared at her burger. She hadn't been on a date in...well, the last date she'd had, if one could call it that, was with Wes in Las Vegas. They'd had sushi and ice cream, then walked the strip for hours, talking. She'd never forget how special Wes had made her feel. He was the only guy she'd ever wanted to give her heart to. And now she found herself battling that same urge again.

But Wes was leaving in only five days.

"Dah!" Sarah-Jane reached for another piece of chicken.

Wes's mouth fell open. "Did you hear that? She just said *daddy*."

Laurel cast him an incredulous look. "Oh, come on, that didn't sound anything like daddy."

"Dah!" Sarah-Jane grinned at Wes, scrunching her nose.

"See." He looked as though he might burst at the seams. Touching his forehead to his daughter's he said, "You did say daddy, didn't you?"

She looked at Laurel then. "Mah!"

"I'm right here, baby."

Sarah-Jane turned to Wes then. "Dah."

This time the word came out more deliberate and sweeter, like a term of endearment, and sent a strange sensation weaving its way through Laurel. Something giddy and exciting filled her, much the way she'd felt when Wes had held her hand that night two years ago. It made her wonder what things might be like if they were a real family. If Wes loved her and she loved him.

Smiling, she captured his attention. "The nearest sushi place is about an hour from Bliss."

His eyes seemed almost riveted to hers. "Sounds perfect to me."

Chapter Sixteen

Wednesday and Thursday passed in a blur as a flurry of activity descended on Irma's. The major work was finally over, and it was time to make the grand old Victorian a home again. Fortunately, plenty of volunteers had shown up, enough that Wes and Laurel had been able to call it a day early Thursday and take Sarah-Jane to the park before throwing some chicken on the grill back at Laurel's. Wes enjoyed those times together, just the three of them. And now that he'd gotten used to them, it was going to make leaving even harder.

At least they still had the weekend, just as soon as they got Irma settled back in.

He stood on Irma's porch with Laurel and Irma, overlooking a yard filled with people who'd pitched in to make this repair go as quickly and smoothly as possible, including Pastor Kleinschmidt and his wife, Paisley, the insurance fellow, the exterminator, and numerous others from the church and community. Wes was in awe of the way the people of Bliss had rallied to help one of their own.

While Wes held Sarah-Jane, Laurel slipped an arm around Irma's shoulders.

"Are you ready to come back home?"

"Oh, I'm more than ready, Laurel." Irma quickly turned her attention to Joyce, who stood on the top step, holding on to the wooden rail. "No offense, Joyce. But as Dorothy said in *The Wizard of Oz*, 'There's no place like home.'"

Laurel moved to the door and took hold of the handle. "In that case, Irma, the place is all yours." Wearing a big smile, she pushed the door open wide.

Wes followed them inside with Sarah-Jane. The once-musty smell of the house had been replaced with the fragrance of fresh paint and something sweet and floral Laurel had plugged into outlets in some of the rooms. "Just wait till you see your brand-new bedroom."

Still in the entry hall, near the base of the stairway, Irma turned to her right and stared through the doorway of her bedroom, her eyes widening as one hand went to her mouth. "This is *my* bedroom?" She stepped tentatively into the space. "It's so beautiful and bright." Her gaze shifted to the corner. "Is that my wedding dress?"

"Yes, ma'am," said Laurel. "It was too pretty to be tucked away in some box."

Reaching for Laurel's hand, Irma grinned. "I never imagined it could look this way. The transformation is like those you see on TV." She hugged Laurel then. "Thank you so much."

"You're welcome." Laurel set the woman away from her. "Paisley and Drenda helped me, along with some other ladies."

"Well, it is just beautiful." Irma chuckled. "Makes me want to take a nap."

"No naps yet." Wes started toward the door. "We have more to show you." He led them into the family room. "I'd never seen a family room with a bathtub in it before—" he turned "—but I think I like this much better."

"This looks like a brand-new room." Irma spun in slow circles.

"All we did was add some fresh paint and move the furniture around a little." Laurel looked at the woman. "I hope you don't mind."

"Mind? I might have to hire you to do the rest of the house."

Wes leaned toward Irma. "Would you like to see what we did with your bathroom?"

"Oh, yes, please."

Laurel helped her up the stairs, then stopped just outside the bathroom door before turning on the light.

Mouth agape, Irma scanned the space. "I was worried the tile might make the room too modern for the house, but this floor looks as though it could have always been here. This is a perfect Victorian bathroom." She looked from Laurel to Wes. "I can't believe the two of you did all of this. You should consider starting a business."

"We had lots of help," Laurel was quick to say. "Which reminds me, we should probably let everyone else in so they can look around."

Things turned into a party then. Paisley and Drenda served up cake and punch on the sideboard in the dining room while people milled about, taking in not only the restoration, but the historic home itself.

Sitting at the dining room table, sharing a piece of cake with Sarah-Jane, Wes experienced a sense of satisfaction he hadn't felt since leaving the military. Was this how he'd feel about his work in Iraq? He'd be helping others, after all, though his heart would definitely be somewhere else.

He snuggled Sarah-Jane closer, then offered her another bite that she readily accepted.

"Mind if I join you?"

Wes looked up to see the pastor easing into the next chair. "Not at all."

"Wes, what you did here is pretty amazing." The man dug his fork into his slice of chocolate cake. "And in just a little over two weeks."

"A job can move much quicker when things fall into place." Like the exterminator and the plumber. "Whenever anyone heard the work was for Irma, they dropped what they were doing and came right here."

"Everybody loves Irma. But you still did the bulk of the work yourself. And this was quite a feat." The pastor set his fork down. "You know, I'm on the board of an organization that aids with rebuilding and disaster efforts right here in Texas. If you decide to come back to the area after Iraq, I'd like to talk with you about it. We could use someone with your skills to help head things up."

An opportunity to do what he loved right here near Laurel and Sarah-Jane? "Yeah, I'd love to know more." His phone buzzed in his pocket just then. Pulling it out, he glanced at the screen. It was Eddie, the man who'd been Wes's spiritual mentor even before he went to work for Servant's Heart. "Excuse me, Pastor. I need to take this."

Standing, he tapped the screen and put the phone to his ear. "Hey, Eddie."

"Are you available to talk for a minute?"

"Yeah, hold on just a second."

Laurel walked into the room just then and offered to take Sarah-Jane.

"Thanks." He smiled at her before heading toward

the door. Outside, he moved around the side of the house. "Sorry about that. What's up?"

"We just realized that there was a mistake on your paperwork. The info they sent you has you starting training here in North Carolina on the fifteenth. It should have said the thirteenth."

Wes's heart sank. "That's only three days from now."

"I know. I wish we'd caught this sooner. I know this is a lot to ask, and we'll work around it if you can't, but is there any way you could be here to start your training on Monday?"

That meant he'd have to leave tomorrow, or early Sunday at the latest, but that would mean driving for eighteen hours straight. He'd done worse in the military, but what about Laurel and Sarah-Jane? He and Laurel had a date tonight.

"I'm not quite sure, Eddie. There are some loose ends I'd need to tie up first, but I'll certainly try."

"At this point, that's all we can ask, Wes. Just holler at me when you know for sure."

"I'll do that." Ending the call, he stared up at the sprawling branches of an old live oak. *God, I'm not ready to say goodbye to Laurel and Sarah-Jane yet.* He'd already been lamenting the fact that his time with them was about to end. How was he going to tell Laurel?

Laurel had probably only had a handful of dates in her life. Throw in the fact that Wes was the father of her child *and* that her feelings for him were already veering out of the friendship lane, and she was doubly nervous about their dinner tonight. She just hoped she could cast those nerves aside long enough to actually enjoy herself.

Glancing across the cab of Wes's pickup, she couldn't

help noticing that Wes looked nervous, too. Something she found rather sweet, not to mention comforting. Though they'd talked during most of their journey, there were times when she'd catch him with his elbow perched on the door and chewing on his thumb.

At the strip center where the restaurant was located, Wes parked his truck, then came around to her side and offered his hand to help her out.

"Thank you." Considering she was wearing a dress, albeit a casual one, she appreciated the gesture. However, the moment her hand touched his, a sharp jolt of awareness shot through her.

"Have I told you how nice you look tonight?" He closed the door behind her without ever releasing her hand.

"Twice." She tucked her hair behind her ear, trying to rein in her suddenly out-of-control emotions.

"That's all?" Continuing toward the restaurant, he added, "I need to step up my game."

"For what it's worth, you look very nice, too." She swept an appreciative gaze over him as he opened the door to the restaurant. He wore a light blue button-down, open at the top, under a navy blazer with dark-wash jeans. The combination of blues made his eyes even more gorgeous than usual.

"Sushi bar or booth?" Behind a narrow podium, the hostess smiled as they entered.

"Booth?" Eyebrows raised, Wes deferred to Laurel.

"Fine by me."

As they followed the twentysomething young lady across the stained-concrete floor, Wes placed a hand against the small of Laurel's back, a simple act that made her feel protected—cherished, even. Something she'd experienced only once before, and it had been Wes who'd made her feel that way then, too.

After waters were delivered and they'd ordered a California roll and some salmon sashimi, Wes rested his forearms on the wooden tabletop. "Okay, I may have told you all of this before, but I just want to make sure I don't forget."

Strange, he didn't usually talk so fast.

"I've set up a payment to your checking account each month for Sarah-Jane, and I've named you as my beneficiary both with Servant's Heart and my life insurance, should something happen."

Nothing like throwing a wet blanket on things. "Wes, I thought this was supposed to be a celebration."

"It is."

She rested her crossed arms on her side of the table and leaned closer. "Things like 'beneficiary' and 'should something happen' are not conducive to a party atmosphere."

"Yeah." Lowering his head, he let out a sigh. "I guess not."

Tilting her head, she eyed him suspiciously. "Is something bothering you?" Perhaps his impending departure was starting to get to him. She certainly didn't want to think about it.

"I'm sorry, Laurel. It has nothing to do with you, though."

With her elbow still on the table, she cradled her neck in her hand. "Okay, so what's wrong?" Wes had helped her talk through her feelings about her father. He'd held her when she cried. She welcomed the chance to support him in return.

He took a sip of his water. A delay tactic if she'd ever seen one. Something was definitely up.

"That phone call I received while we were at Irma's this morning. It was from Servant's Heart. Seems someone messed up. I'm supposed to start my training Monday, not Wednesday, as stated on my paperwork."

Her insides tightened. "But you're not leaving until Monday."

"They've asked me to try to make it to North Carolina by Monday."

Indignation sparked inside her. "How can they do that, though? The mistake was theirs, not yours."

"I know. But that doesn't mean they can't ask."

Laurel watched the man across from her. Wes was a man of his word, committed to whatever he did. "And you feel as though you should try to accommodate them."

He dragged a hand through his hair. "I don't want to go any earlier than I'd originally planned. The thought of leaving you and Sarah-Jane is already eating me alive."

In which case, she was probably only adding to his misery. "Are you leaving tomorrow, then?"

"No. I want more time with Sarah-Jane." Reaching across the table, he grabbed Laurel's hand. "And you." His determined gaze bore into hers, making a lump the size of Texas lodge in her throat.

"California roll." The waiter set the first plate on the table as Wes let go of Laurel's hand. "And salmon sashimi." After depositing the plate, he looked from Laurel to Wes. "Anything else?"

Wes forced a smile. "Not right now, thank you."

Watching Wes, Laurel removed her chopsticks from their paper sleeve, her appetite waning. "What are your plans, then?"

He moved his napkin to his lap. "To spend tomorrow with you and Sarah-Jane, then head out first thing Sunday morning."

Pinching a slice of the California roll between her chopsticks, she looked at him. "How long of a drive is it?"

"Eighteen hours. Give or take."

She dropped the roll and the sticks on her plate. "Wes, you can't drive that straight through. That's insane."

"I'll take breaks."

"That doesn't take the place of sleep."

"Laurel, I was in the military, remember? There were times I was up forty-eight hours straight."

"Yes. But you were probably in a war zone, surrounded by the enemy or something."

He laughed.

"What?"

"You have an active imagination."

"Only because I care about you."

"That's good to know. Because I care about you, too. So why don't we change the subject and try to enjoy ourselves. Like you said, this is supposed to be a celebration, after all. And I can't think of anything better to celebrate than being with you."

Laurel wasn't sure she knew what a swoon was or if one could do it sitting down, but looking into Wes's amazing blue eyes right now, she was pretty sure she was swooning.

They changed the topic and spent the rest of their meal discussing Sarah-Jane and how well things had come together at Irma's. Not to mention that crazy dinner they'd shared with Joyce and Irma. By the time they left the restaurant, they were laughing and holding hands once again.

"Look." Wes pointed toward the western horizon as they reached his truck.

Shades of pink and orange colored the sky. "What a beautiful sunset."

"Mmm-hmm."

When she looked at Wes, he was staring at her.

"But it pales in comparison to you."

Her heart beat a staccato in her chest as his hand cupped her cheek. She swallowed hard as his eyes searched hers. Was he going to—?

Before she could finish her thought—wish, perhaps—his lips touched hers. Tenderly, yet thoroughly, he kissed her. Right there in the parking lot for all the world to see. And all she could think about was how she was falling for this man. How he made her want things she never dared to dream of before. How— Her phone rang.

Reluctantly tearing herself away from Wes, she located the phone in her purse and pulled it out to look at the screen. "It's my father." She swiped the screen. "Hello."

"Laurel, honey." A ragged breath came through the line. "I'm sorry, but I'm afraid I'm not going to make it out there tonight like I was hoping."

"Oh." Disappointment pricked at her. "Do you know when you might make it back?"

"No, I don't. Things have gotten a little crazy here, and I just..." His voice trailed off. "I'll keep you posted, though."

The same heart that had been soaring moments ago went into a tailspin. The man could make all the promises he wanted, but Laurel knew the truth. Her father wasn't coming back. Not today, not ever.

She eyed the man beside her. Wes was leaving, too.

What if he decided not to come back? Even if he did, would it be for Sarah-Jane or would he want Laurel, too?

Blowing out a breath, she tucked her phone back in her purse, wondering if that was a risk she was willing to take.

Chapter Seventeen

Wes had had such high hopes for this evening. And everything had been going so well until Laurel got that call from Jimmy. Naturally, she tried to act as if his delayed return didn't bother her, but Wes knew better. Their chatter wasn't near as lively as it had been on the way to the restaurant. He did his best to keep it going as they made the drive home, but then Laurel would grow quiet and simply stare out her window.

When he pulled his truck into her drive less than an hour after they'd left the restaurant, he killed the engine before helping Laurel out of the vehicle.

"Thanks." This time, she promptly let go of his hand and started toward the porch.

"Y'all are back early." Rae was sitting on the living room floor, playing with a pajama-clad Sarah-Jane. "I wasn't expecting you for another couple of hours."

Moving around the sofa, Laurel smiled at the two of them. The first smile Wes had seen since her father called. "That would explain why someone is up past her bedtime."

"We've been having a great time." Rae looked up at them. "We ate macaroni and cheese, we sang, we danced. 'Baby Shark' makes for a very good workout, you know."

"I can imagine," said Laurel. "Except now it's going to be stuck in your head for who knows how long."

"Yeah, you're probably right." Rae stood as Sarah-Jane spotted Wes.

The child pushed to her feet and toddled toward him as fast as her wobbly legs would allow. And Wes's heart swelled faster than the Grinch's when he discovered the true meaning of Christmas.

He scooped his daughter into his arms and inhaled the sweet smell of baby shampoo. That was one of many simple pleasures he was going to miss when he left. Stepping over toys, he carried her to the glider near the fireplace and sat down while Laurel and Rae resumed their discussion of the events at Irma's this morning.

Once he set the chair into motion, Sarah-Jane didn't seem to mind. Instead of trying to get down, she yawned and snuggled against him.

"Wes doesn't even live here—" his sister shot him a glance "—and I've already had people inquiring about how long he's going to be in town because they've got projects they'd like him to tackle."

"How would they even know?" He eyed Rae.

"Small town," said Laurel. "Word gets around fast, and reputations are everything."

"In that case, Rae, you can tell them I'm scheduling for next summer."

"Well, considering that Mason Krebbs is about their only option, I could probably have you booked up in no time."

"It's definitely something I'll keep in mind." Though it wouldn't be service oriented, like he preferred. But he could talk to the pastor about the organization he'd mentioned.

Laurel looked at Wes with a half smile, half pout. "Looks like someone was more tuckered out than she thought."

He lowered his gaze to see a sleeping Sarah-Jane.

"I can take her." Laurel started toward him.

"That's okay." He snuggled his daughter closer. "I'd like to hold her awhile longer."

"I have a feeling I'll conk out pretty quick once I get still, too." Rae retrieved her purse from the counter. "You two enjoy the rest of your evening." She hugged Laurel before leaving.

After closing the door, Laurel crossed the room to come alongside Wes. She stroked Sarah-Jane's head. "So precious."

He couldn't stop looking at his daughter. "Yes, she is. Leaving her is going to be the hardest thing I've ever done." Turning his attention to Laurel, he added, "It's tearing me up just thinking about it."

"I guess we'll have to get those video chats going as soon as we can."

"I'm not very computer savvy, so I might need a tutorial."

"It's not that bad. We'll go over things tomorrow." Her focus returned to Sarah-Jane. "I should probably put her in bed now."

"Would you mind if I did it?"

She blinked twice. "No, not at all."

Standing along with him, Laurel remained in the living room while he carried his daughter down the hall to her room.

Before laying her in her crib, he placed his mouth near her ear and whispered, "I love you, Sarah-Jane.

Don't you ever doubt that." He kissed her soft cheek. "Sleep well, sweetheart."

As he laid her down, he marveled at the way she rolled onto her side, her hands coming together as though she were praying.

His eyes burned. *God, You've granted me such precious gifts in Laurel and Sarah-Jane. And now I have to walk away. I know it's temporary, but I'm going to need Your help to get me through this next year.*

Moving into the hall, he pulled the door to before returning to the main part of the house, where he saw Laurel in the kitchen, cradling a mug of something steamy. She looked as though she'd been crying. Was she still upset about that phone call from her father? Or was it something more?

"She's out like a light," he said as he entered the room.

"I'm sure Rae wore her out." She set her cup on the counter. "Are you going to head out?"

Approaching the kitchen, his heart tightened. Did she want him to go? "I was hoping to spend a little more time with you."

After a deep breath, she nodded. "I fixed myself some herbal tea. Can I get you something?"

Yeah, the Laurel he'd had a wonderful time with at the restaurant. "No, I'm good." Or more like disappointed. Nervous.

With the peninsula between them, he said, "About your father."

Her sad eyes met his.

"Saying goodbye to you was as tough on him as it was on you."

She clasped her mug so tightly, her knuckles were white. "How do you know that?"

"Did you not see the pain in his eyes? But he has a business to run. Things happen. I'm sure he'll be back just as soon as he can."

She removed the tea bag from the steaming cup and tossed it into the trash. "You're probably right." Whisking past him, she moved to the table and pulled out a chair.

Not exactly what he'd had in mind. The sofa was definitely cozier, but he could let it go for now.

"Did you hear what Irma said today? About hiring me—us—to redo the rest of her house." A nervous chuckle escaped her pretty lips.

"She also said that we should consider starting a business." He watched Laurel, hoping his next statement would help him get a better read on her. "What would you think about that?"

"I think that would be impossible since you're going to Iraq." Cradling her mug, she took a sip.

"What about when I get back?"

She set her cup on the table. "Does that mean you're planning to come back to Bliss?"

He wanted to think he saw a glimmer of hope in her eyes. "Absolutely. Sarah-Jane is my daughter, and I plan to be a father to her. The only way I can truly do that is to be here for her."

Laurel gave a curt nod. "She'll like that."

"It's more than just that, though."

"Oh?"

"Laurel, spending time with you these past few weeks, seeing how well we work together… What I'm trying to say is that I care about you. You're important to me. And I was hoping that, maybe when I get back, we could talk about giving our daughter the kind of family she deserves. You know, a mother *and* a father. Together."

Her eyes searched his for the longest time until he finally said, "Tell me what you're thinking, Laurel."

Standing, she crossed to the kitchen. "I'm sorry, Wes. Sarah-Jane and I are not some sort of package deal where you can get two for the price of one. Yes, I want Sarah-Jane to have an ongoing relationship with you. But you and me?" She wagged a finger between them. "That's not going to happen."

Wes felt as though he'd been punched in the gut. Staring blankly at the table, he wasn't sure what to say or do. Should he stay and try to plead his case? Or should he just leave?

"I think you should go," Laurel said, giving him the answer he hadn't wanted or even expected.

Just a couple of hours ago, things were going so well. Laurel had been in his arms and seemingly wanted to be there. Now…

Was it the phone call from her father that had shifted things? Had she convinced herself that Wes wasn't coming back, even though he'd told her he was?

Shoving his chair away from the table, he stood, his heart aching as much as it had when he'd learned of his parents' deaths. He paused in front of her on his way to the door. "Good night, Laurel."

She looked away, and Wes found himself wondering what he was going to do now.

Laurel woke up on the couch the next morning, feeling as though her eyes were filled with grit. From the monitor on the side table behind her, she could hear her daughter happily jabbering—the same way she'd heard Wes telling Sarah-Jane that he loved her.

If only he loved Laurel, too, last night could have turned out so much different. Instead, Wes had just assumed that since he was Sarah-Jane's father, Laurel would automatically agree to marry him.

The thought made her heart ache anew. Wes might care about her, but she wasn't important enough to love.

"Mah!" Sarah-Jane's voice grew louder, and Laurel smiled.

There was one person who loved her, though. One precious little girl that Laurel wouldn't trade for the world.

Still wearing her dress from last night, she stood and stretched before continuing down the hall to Sarah-Jane's room. "Good morning, sunshine."

Sarah-Jane's smile was big as she bounced up and down, holding on to the side of the crib.

"Looks like you've got plenty of energy today." Too bad Laurel couldn't say the same. She'd spent much of the night either crying or chastising herself for doing so until she finally fell asleep in the living room. Even now it frustrated her. Wes was not worth losing sleep over. Yet no matter how many times she told herself that, things kept shooting through her head, reminding her to the contrary.

After changing Sarah-Jane's diaper, Laurel set her daughter on the floor and followed her down the hall. Her walking was getting better, and she was finally reaching the point where she preferred walking over crawling.

About the time they made it to the kitchen, there was a knock at the door, and Laurel's whole being tensed. What if it was Wes? This was his last day in Bliss, after all, and he'd said he wanted to spend the day with

Sarah-Jane. Okay, so he'd included Laurel in that, too, but now she knew she was nothing but extra baggage.

She sucked in a breath and moved to the door, praying her eyes weren't too puffy. The last thing she wanted was for Wes to think she'd been crying over him. Even if it was the truth.

When she opened the door, though, it wasn't Wes standing there, but her father.

Feeling more than a little befuddled, she said, "What—? I thought—"

"Soon as I hung up with you, I realized that if I waited until everything was under control, I might never make it back here. Laurel, you're more important to me than any ol' business. So I left instructions with my crew, hopped in my truck and drove until I got to Bliss."

She simply stood there with her mouth hanging open. "But what about your heart? Don't you know you need your rest?"

"I called the Bliss Inn on my way out of Midland so they'd have a room waiting for me when I got in."

"Which was?"

"Somewhere around two. So yes, I got some sleep. But I couldn't wait to see you."

Tears filled Laurel's eyes, spilling onto her cheeks.

"Oh, Laurel." He stepped inside, the aromas of coffee and soap enveloping her right along with his arms.

For the first time in her life—that she could remember, anyway—she hugged him back with all of her might. These past few weeks had been such an emotional roller coaster, and now everything had finally caught up to her, including one freshly broken heart. "God must have known I needed a daddy today." The words were muffled against his chest.

Just then, she felt Sarah-Jane at her leg. She pulled away to see unshed tears in her father's eyes, too.

She picked up her daughter. "Do you remember your pawpaw?"

Sarah-Jane laid her head against Laurel's shoulder.

Jimmy smoothed a hand across her back. "That's all right. We'll have time to get to know each other." His eyes moved to Laurel. "Now what did you mean when you said you needed a daddy?"

Her bottom lip pooched out as fresh tears welled. "I'll tell you over coffee."

A short time later, she and her father sat across from each other at the table, each nursing a cup of fresh brew, while Sarah-Jane nibbled on a banana in her high chair. And Laurel opened up about last night.

"We went on a date, and it was probably the best time I've had since…well, since the last time Wes and I went out." Even Wes's kiss had held such promise. "Then when he was putting Sarah-Jane to bed, I heard him on the monitor, telling her how much he loved her."

"Is that a bad thing?"

"No. But he doesn't love me."

Her father winced. "He said that?"

"His exact words were that he cares about me and I'm important to him. Then he went on to suggest that when he gets back next year, he and I should 'talk about giving our daughter the kind of family she deserves.' With 'a mother *and* a father.' As if that was the only reason we should be together."

"So you think he's considering a loveless marriage for the sake of Sarah-Jane?"

"That's what it sounded like to me. I mean, there was no mention of love or wanting to be with me. Only Sarah-Jane."

"Laurel, have you told Wes how you feel about him?"

"I told him I cared about him."

"I'd venture to say you're in love with him."

Her shoulders sagged. "I am. But I'm not going to tell him that. If he told me first, that would be one thing, but—"

"Have you stopped to think that maybe he's just as afraid to tell you as you are to tell him?"

"Whose side are you on?"

"Yours. Always. That's why I don't want you to throw away something precious the way I did. I didn't come back for you because I was afraid your mother had found someone else and would send me packing. It wasn't until I had nothing to lose that I finally found you, and things turned out better than I ever imagined." He stared into his now empty cup. "Laurel, I'd hate to see you let fear keep you from your dreams, especially since I'm fairly certain Wes loves you, too."

Tilting her head left and right, trying to work the kinks out of her neck, she said, "It's Sarah-Jane he loves. Not me."

"Are you sure? Or are you just afraid to find out? I've seen the way he looks at you, the way he protected you when I showed up." Her father eyed her across the table. "It's not all about Sarah-Jane. It's about you."

I've never forgotten you, Laurel. Wes had said that the day he asked her about Sarah-Jane's name. Could it be true? Could she have lingered in Wes's mind the way he had hers?

"Let me give you something else to think about."

She looked at her father. "What's that?"

"Do you want Wes to leave thinking that you don't love him?"

"No." She tried to focus on her daughter so she wouldn't cry. "But I'm scared."

"Can't be any worse than what happened last night."

The man had a point.

God, it is so not like me to do something like that. Should I?

"I'd be happy to watch my granddaughter if you'd like to pay him a visit."

It sounded like she had her answer.

A giddy, nauseous feeling began to swell in her belly. "Okay, I'll do it."

After scrubbing her face, pulling her hair into a ponytail and donning some yoga pants and a cute tunic, she thanked her father and headed to Rae's.

Just about every parking spot was taken as people filed in for a leisurely Saturday breakfast, but she managed to snag the last one. Then, with a fortifying breath, she willed herself through the doors of the Fresh Start Café and marched straight to the back and the stairs that led to Rae's apartment.

"Laurel?"

She turned at the sound of Rae's voice.

Coffeepot in hand, her friend continued toward her. "What's up?"

"I need to talk to Wes."

Rae's expression went blank. "I guess you haven't talked to him."

"Not since last night."

"He left for North Carolina before sunup. He's gone, Laurel."

Chapter Eighteen

Wes walked across the parking lot of the Servant's Heart headquarters Monday morning, feeling as though he'd had the life sucked out of him. While the eighteen-hour drive had been uneventful, he was a mess. His insides hadn't been this knotted up in years. While leaving Sarah-Jane had been challenging enough, hearing Laurel say there was no future for them had cut him to the quick. What had changed her mind? Or had he read her wrong all along?

For the thousandth time, he thought about their kiss. From where he stood, she'd been all in on it...until her phone rang, anyway. Could that have had something to do with her pushing him away? Her conversation with Jimmy had definitely dampened her mood. Could that call have caused her feelings of rejection to resurface?

Except Wes hadn't rejected her. He'd told her that he cared about her and that he wanted them to be together. The only thing he hadn't done was tell her he loved her. Yet instead of going back and confessing his true feelings, he'd hightailed it out of Bliss early the next morning without so much as a goodbye to Laurel or Sarah-Jane. A fact that had him kicking himself halfway across the country. Would it have made a difference, though?

He dragged a hand through his hair. It wasn't like he was adept at understanding women. So when one finally broke through the wall he'd built and actually captured his heart, it figured that he'd blow it.

Passing through the double glass doors of the large, relatively modern office building, into the reception area, he hoped he looked better than he felt. Because he felt as though he'd been run over by a tank.

A young woman smiled as he approached the reception desk. "How can I help you?"

"I'm here to meet with Eddie Perkins."

She took Wes's name then told him to take a seat while she let Eddie know he was there.

Perhaps it was good he'd be seeing his old friend today. He and Eddie had always been close and Wes appreciated his friend's perspective on things. Once Wes told him all that had transpired in the past few weeks, his friend was certain to have some sage advice.

Easing into a padded chair, Wes stared blankly out of the floor-to-ceiling windows, wondering what Laurel and Sarah-Jane were doing. Probably finishing up breakfast. They were an hour behind him, after all. How he longed to see his baby girl. But what would that look like now? Laurel would be a part of any video chat. Sitting on the other side of the screen, staring at her beautiful face, knowing she would never be his. How awkward was that going to be?

Before Wes had time to contemplate the magazines on the table beside him, Eddie came around the corner.

"Wes." Arms wide, he approached as Wes stood.

"Good to see you," Wes said as the two briefly hugged.

"You, too." Releasing him, Eddie studied Wes. "You're looking kinda rough, though. You must have really jumped through some hoops to get here."

Wes rubbed the back of his neck. "I'm not gonna kid you. It's been a rough couple of days."

"Let's go to my office so we can talk."

Wes followed his friend across the tiled lobby, down a carpeted hallway and into a rather generic office, save for the family and military photos that lined one wall.

Eddie motioned for Wes to take one of two chairs in front of the desk, while Eddie continued to his office chair. "So how have you been? What have you been up to?"

Pondering all that had transpired in the last three weeks, Wes shook his head. "Well, for starters, I've just recently learned that I have a daughter. I don't know if that's going to be a problem for the organization or not, the fact that I wasn't married to her mother."

Forearms resting on his desk, Eddie studied him. "No wonder you're so messed up."

"Saying goodbye to that little girl was one of the toughest things I've ever done, especially since I just met her."

"How old is she?"

"Just turned fifteen months."

"Oh, so she's little."

"Yeah. Cute as a bug, too." He pulled his phone from his pocket, brought up a picture and showed it to Eddie. "Her name is Sarah-Jane."

Eddie leaned in to look at the screen. "What a doll. She's got your eyes."

A sense of pride swept through him. "I got to see her take her first steps." That was also the first time Laurel had referred to him as *daddy*.

"Where does her mother fit into this picture?"

"I'm not sure." Wes leaned back in the chair. "Laurel is the only woman I've ever been drawn to. And while I've always said I don't deserve a family, now I want it so bad I can taste it."

"Are you saying you love Sarah-Jane's mother?"

He thought about the way he felt when he was with Laurel. And how horrible he'd felt since he'd left. "I think so. Yes."

"Any idea how she feels about you?"

"That's what's got me so confused." Resting his elbows on his knees, he went over the ups and downs of their relationship, before sharing the events of Friday night.

"Wes, do you think Laurel is worth fighting for?"

"Without a doubt."

Eddie leaned back in his own chair, clasping his hands behind his head as he contemplated everything Wes had shared. A move Wes recognized from their time together in the military.

"To answer your first question," Eddie began, "I don't think you fathering this child will be a problem for the organization. We've all sinned. If not, we wouldn't need Jesus. What I'm wondering, though, is if this job is still a good fit for you. Your life has changed a lot and rather suddenly. You have a little girl who needs her father. So, perhaps, this position isn't the best fit for you anymore."

"But I made a commitment."

Straightening, he turned his chair, so he was looking straight at Wes. "And what about your commitment to your daughter?" Hands clasped tightly, his gaze bore into Wes's. "Being a father is the greatest gift you could be given."

His friend's intensity had Wes sitting taller. "I'm aware of that, sir. Trust me, I don't take this lightly."

"And what about her mother? Are you just going to let her slip through your hands? Or are you ready to fight for that family, I believe, God wants you to have?"

Wes had been gone for a week, and Laurel still missed him. Countless times she'd reached for her phone, determined to call him and tell him that she loved him. Yet each and every time she'd stopped herself. The man was preparing to go overseas, and she didn't want anything to distract him from his mission.

Besides, he hadn't called her, either—well, Sarah-Jane, anyway. Laurel knew he must be missing his daughter. He was probably just busy with his training.

With Irma's house complete, and Wes and her father gone, Laurel had tried to return to her usual routine. It was nice to make her morning trips for coffee again but, other than that, things just felt…different.

Her life had changed so drastically in the last few weeks. Things she'd once only dreamed of—a father, falling in love—had, by the grace of God, found their way into her life. And while neither had come without trepidation, she wouldn't trade them for the world.

She and her father had spoken every day since his return to Midland on Tuesday. Not only had they made a promise to be open about their feelings, he was worried about her. And Laurel couldn't help thinking how good it felt to have someone, family, who cared.

She'd also spent a lot of time thinking about her grandmother this week. The woman had truly loved Laurel, in her own misguided way. And without Grandmama Corwin, Laurel never would have found her way to Bliss, where her life had taken on so much more meaning.

If only Wes were here. Apparently the old adage "absence makes the heart grow fonder" was true, because there wasn't a moment that had gone by that she didn't think about him.

"Mah."

Standing in the kitchen, Laurel looked down at her daughter, who was trying in vain to open the cabinet door.

"I knew those child locks would come in handy someday." She knelt beside Sarah-Jane. "Sorry, baby. There are things in there that could hurt you."

Sarah-Jane smiled and began to bounce.

"Let me finish restocking your diaper bag and then we'll go to the farmers market, okay?" Standing again, she snagged a couple of snacks from the pantry, carefully hiding them from those watchful blue eyes that seemed to have grown keenly aware of the portal that contained a certain little person's favorite treats.

After adding them to her bag, she snatched it up and started for the front door to put it in the stroller before loading Sarah-Jane.

"I'll be right back, baby." She moved around the peninsula, continuing into the living room. But when she opened the door, her heart skidded to a stop.

"Wes?" Standing there, dumbfounded, she found herself clinging to the knob as a thrill sprang to life inside her, though angst and doubt quickly tried to overtake it. "What are you doing here?" Well, that was a stupid question. "I mean, let me get Sarah-Jane." She started to turn.

"I'm not here because of Sarah-Jane."

A lump formed in her throat as she faced him again.

"I'm here because of you, Laurel. You captured my heart the moment I saw you at that pool two years ago, and no matter how hard I've tried to dismiss or forget you, I can't."

She had to be dreaming. Wes was in North Carolina.

She squeezed her eyes shut. But when she opened them, he was still there on her porch, hands dangling from the pockets of his faded jeans.

"Dah!"

Laurel turned at the sound of her daughter's voice. "You heard your daddy, didn't you?"

Spotting her father, Sarah-Jane's pace quickened. Arms in the air, she grinned as she beelined toward him. Until she lost her balance.

"Uh-oh." Wes stepped inside, scooping Sarah-Jane into his arms before she hit the floor. "Got a little too much forward thrust going on there."

"She's excited to see you." Truth be known, Laurel was, too. She watched as her daughter laid her head against Wes's shoulder.

Wes patted her back, his attention returning to Laurel. "That night we had dinner with Irma and Joyce, I told you my dream of finding the perfect partner died along with my parents. But since spending time with you, that dream has been resurrected."

Tears pricked the backs of her eyes. Could this really be happening? Was Wes really saying these words to her?

"I'm back in Bliss for good, Laurel, in hopes that I can win your heart. I love you, and I'd like nothing more than for us to be a family. You, me and Sarah-Jane."

Emotions threatened to overtake her. She'd never heard such words directed at her. And the amount of joy vibrating through her being was almost more than she could stand.

With her heart racing, she stared at this man she loved more than anything. "But what if I want more babies?"

His grin went from hesitant to certain. "Then I'm in for that, too. Whatever God has in store for us." He slipped an arm around her waist and pulled her close. "So long as I get to share every moment of it with you."

Placing her hand over his heart, she felt it pounding every bit as wildly as her own. She peered up at him. "My heart already belongs to you, Wes. I love you, too."

He lowered his head and kissed her as thoroughly as he could with Sarah-Jane in his arms. When they parted, he said, "You hear that, Sarah-Jane? We're going to be a family." He tossed their daughter in the air before setting her on the floor. Straightening, he cupped Laurel's cheeks in his hands and stared into her eyes. "You are the greatest gift I've ever been given. Will you marry me?"

With happy tears streaming down her cheeks and her heart overflowing with joy, she smiled bigger than ever before. "In a heartbeat."

Epilogue

"What do you think, Sarah-Jane?" Standing in the glow of hundreds of tiny white lights, Laurel smiled at the wide-eyed child tucked in her father's arms. "Our first Christmas tree as a family."

"And in our new house," Wes was quick to add.

Laurel looked around the spacious room with vaulted ceilings. "When we came here back in April for dinner with Joyce and Irma, I never would have guessed I'd be living here."

"You mean that *we'd* be living here."

Deciding she wanted to be near her children in Dallas, Joyce had come to Laurel and Wes even before their September wedding and offered them her house, saying, "It's the perfect home for a family."

Of course, as soon as Wes heard it was on an acre and half and there was already an outbuilding he could use as a shop, he was sold. Then he learned Joyce had offered it to them at well below market value. After updating the kitchen and bathrooms, not to mention going through gallons of greige paint to cover that dark wood paneling, the home had turned out to be perfect for them. An office plus four bedrooms meant they had room to grow.

"All that's missing now," said Wes, "are the ornaments."

As if on cue, the doorbell rang.

Laurel feigned a gasp. "Who's here, Sarah-Jane?"

The three of them made their way to the door. Laurel and Wes knew that no tree-trimming party would be complete without the rest of their family.

"Merry Christmas!" Rae, Paisley and Christa cheered collectively as Laurel opened the door.

"Merry Christmas to you." Laurel hugged each of them as they entered.

Rae promptly kissed her niece while a Santa hat–clad Christa held up two bottles of sparkling cider.

"Where should I put these?"

"The refrigerator is good for now." Laurel started to close the door.

"Wait for me."

She yanked it back open. "Hey, Dad."

Almost three months ago, he'd walked her down the aisle, making two of Laurel's dreams come true at one time. He'd also sold his business in Midland and moved to Bliss shortly after that and was now living in Laurel's old house, where she could keep him under a watchful eye. Fortunately, his congestive heart failure was in the early stages, and getting out from under the stress of his business had greatly improved his blood pressure. Now all she could do was monitor his diet and pray that God would grant them as much time together as possible.

"Looks like it's time to get this party started." Wes set Sarah-Jane on the floor and followed her as she ran back into the family room.

"Would you like to eat these now or later?" Beside

Laurel, Paisley motioned to the beautiful tray of cookies she'd brought.

"Now. Definitely."

They all moved into the family room, where Sarah-Jane stared up at the illuminated tree.

"Before we get started—" Laurel grabbed a sparkling bag from the kitchen counter "—I have something for each of you." One by one, she handed each of their guests a wrapped bundle. "I wanted every member of our family to have an ornament on our tree."

"Can we open them?" Anticipation filled Rae's voice.

"Of course." Laurel had chosen ornaments suited to each person. Rae's was a glittering cup of coffee, Christa's a shimmering tool belt. Paisley received a stylishly dressed baker holding a plate of cookies, while Jimmy's was an oil derrick.

"This is perfect." Her father chuckled as he held it up for inspection.

Reaching into the bag, Laurel pulled out one final box. "And I have one more for Sarah-Jane." She handed it to her daughter, who was now sitting in her daddy's lap on the floor. "Why don't you help her, Wes?"

"All right. Let's see what we got, Sarah-Jane." He tore one end open, allowing his daughter to take over from there.

Anticipation rose inside Laurel.

Finally, he pulled out the ornament with two teddy bears sitting atop a rocking horse. "Look at that, sweetheart." He held it up for her to see. "It says Big Sister."

Notes of "White Christmas" played softly in the background as everyone except for Wes fell quiet.

"What do you think about that, Sarah-Jane? Shall we put it on the tree?"

Laurel held her breath, trying not to laugh. She

glanced at her father, Rae, Christa and Paisley, who were all doing the same. Obviously Laurel's little hint was lost on her husband.

Helping Sarah-Jane hang her ornament, he said, "See there, someday you're going to be a big sist—" Slowly he turned to face Laurel. "Wait. Does this mean…?"

Laurel nodded. "You've got until July to get the nursery ready."

A nanosecond later, he swooped her up in his arms and kissed her.

"Now this calls for a celebration," she heard Paisley say. "Christa, pop the top on that sparkling cider."

When Wes finally allowed Laurel's feet to again touch the ground, he cupped her cheek and stared at her with an intensity that made her heart race. "I love you so much."

"I love you, too."

Moments later, Rae lifted her glass. "A toast to my brother and my best friends."

Surrounded by all the people she loved, Laurel's heart overflowed. God had been so gracious to her. He'd heard the prayers of a lonely heart and given her the family she'd always longed for. And that was the greatest gift she'd ever been given.

* * * * *

Dear Reader,

Have you ever made a mistake? Sometimes those mistakes impact our lives and the lives of others. The good news is that God can turn even our biggest mistakes into our greatest blessings.

I loved getting to know Wes and Laurel and watching these two wounded souls discover their hearts' desires. And Sarah-Jane was an absolute delight. I hope you enjoyed your first visit to Bliss, Texas, where life moves at a slower pace and traditional values still abound. Having moved from the suburbs of Dallas–Fort Worth to a small rural community three years ago, I share Laurel's appreciation for a simpler way of life.

I'm looking forward to sharing more Bliss with you as we delve into the lives of Laurel's friends, Christa, Paisley and Rae. Until then, I would love to hear from you. You can contact me via my website, mindyobenhaus.com, or you can snail-mail me c/o Love Inspired Books, 195 Broadway, 24th floor, New York, NY 10007.

Wishing you many blessings,
Mindy

SPECIAL EXCERPT FROM

HQN

After police officer Drew Martin loses his sight in an accident, it takes all he has to face his ex-wife—and the feelings she still stirs in him. But for the sake of their teen daughters, who are struggling with some very real issues, he'll relocate to their Chesapeake Bay town. Together, can they find a way to repair their fractured family?

Read on for a peek at
Reunion at the Shore*, the next emotional and heartwarming book in* USA TODAY *bestselling author Lee Tobin McClain's The Off Season series!*

Sunday afternoon, Drew walked into the motel lobby, Navy at his side, feeling wary.

He'd planned to talk to Ria once she got home from church, figure out what to do about living here and about Kaitlyn's upcoming release from the hospital. But before he could have that conversation, while he'd been walking Navy, Ria had called out from the motel lobby, asking him to come to some sort of a meeting. He didn't know who would be there or what the meeting was about, except that it related to Kaitlyn.

More than anything else in the world, he wanted to help his daughter. He'd committed to stay in town for the next few months at least. But the truth was, he was a disabled stranger in a strange town, with no job. Right at this moment, going into a situation where he didn't know what to expect…yeah. He was definitely on edge.

"There's a couch two feet to your right." Ria was suddenly standing next to him, and he felt a sharp tingle of awareness. Her slightly husky voice, the flowery perfume she wore—they had always had their effect on him. Plus there was the fact that she was beautiful and didn't even know it.

Thinking of her beauty stabbed him, because he couldn't see it. Couldn't read the expression on her face, couldn't watch her tilt back her head when she laughed, couldn't look into her eyes.

The loss pressed down on him, making it hard to breathe.

He sucked in air, pushed the negative thoughts away and sat down, and Ria sat next to him. After a short, quiet bark, Navy settled at his feet.

There were multiple reasons he didn't want to stay on at the motel, but Ria was one of them. He'd have to face the fact that he was still attracted to her, but she didn't want him and didn't love him. He hadn't been enough for her when they'd married and he definitely wasn't enough for her now.

"Do you want to talk about Kait's schooling now?" he asked Ria once the meeting was over.

"You really could stay here, you know," she said instead of answering his question.

"It wouldn't be good."

There was a pause. "Sure, I guess."

He heard the hurt in her voice. Maybe it was the emotions of the day, but he reached out and pulled her closer, into a hug, patting her back and, he had to admit to himself, enjoying the way she felt there.

Which was the problem. "It's too hard to be this close together," he growled into that familiar neck, and he felt her body respond in the way it always did, moving marginally closer and settling perfectly against him.

He'd ached to hold her, and now that he was doing it, the memories flooded him. From the first time he'd kissed her, young and full of bravado, pretending arrogance but secretly afraid, to the last time, when he'd put everything he had into it, hoping to save their marriage.

They stayed that way for a moment, and then she tugged loose. "Maybe it's better if you do go," she said.

"Yeah. Listen, let's both think about this a little and then I'll give you a call." He was trying to keep his tone cool, but it wasn't working.

And it would be best to get a little distance from Ria, but that sure wasn't what he felt like doing.